///////// N*SC*R

SECRETS and LEGENDS

TAILSPIN
by Michele Dunaway

From the opening green flag at Daytona to the final checkered flag at Homestead, the competition will be fierce for the NASCAR Sprint Cup Series championship.

The **Grosso** family practically has engine oil in their veins. For them racing represents not just a way of life but a tradition that goes back to NASCAR's inception. Like all families, they also have a few skeletons to hide. What happens when someone peeks inside the closet becomes a matter that threatens to destroy them.

The **Murphys** have been supporting drivers in the pits for generations, despite a vendetta with the Grossos that's almost as old as NASCAR itself! But the Murphys have their own secrets... and a few indiscretions that could cost them everything.

The **Branches** are newcomers, and some would say upstarts. But as this affluent Texas family is further enmeshed in the world of NASCAR, they become just as embroiled in the intrigues on and off the track.

The **Motor Media Group** are the PR people responsible for the positive public perception of NASCAR's stars. They are the glue that repairs the damage. And more than anything, they feel the brunt of the backlash....

These NASCAR families have secrets to hide, and reputations to protect. This season will test them all.

Dear Reader,

NASCAR is my favorite sport. When it hooks you, you're a fan for life. Race weekends you'll find me tuned to my TV set, or if I'm lucky, I'm at the track.

For Terri Whalen, NASCAR racing is her life. She's a driver at heart, but since her career didn't pan out, she's turned her attention to other jobs that keep her at the track every weekend. Max Harper loves NASCAR, but his work keeps him busy and he hasn't been to a race in years.

That old adage says that opposites attract, and in Max and Terri's case it's true. Neither plans to ever settle down again. But when fate speaks, they discover they have to listen and heed its call.

I can't express how wonderful it's been to work with such a talented group of authors on this continuity series. I've enjoyed creating this fictional world and bringing Max and Terri's love story to life against such an exciting backdrop.

As always, please feel free to contact me through the link at my Web site, www.micheledunaway.com.

Let your heart race,

Michele Dunaway

NASCAR

TAILSPIN

Michele Dunaway

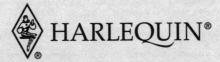

HARLEQUIN®

TORONTO • NEW YORK • LONDON
AMSTERDAM • PARIS • SYDNEY • HAMBURG
STOCKHOLM • ATHENS • TOKYO • MILAN • MADRID
PRAGUE • WARSAW • BUDAPEST • AUCKLAND

ISBN-13: 978-0-373-21794-6
ISBN-10:   0-373-21794-3

TAILSPIN

Copyright © 2008 by Harlequin Books S.A.

Michele Dunaway is acknowledged as the author of this work.

NASCAR® and the NASCAR Library Collection are registered trademarks of the National Association for Stock Car Auto Racing, Inc.

All rights reserved. Except for use in any review, the reproduction or utilization of this work in whole or in part in any form by any electronic, mechanical or other means, now known or hereafter invented, including xerography, photocopying and recording, or in any information storage or retrieval system, is forbidden without the written permission of the publisher, Harlequin Enterprises Limited, 225 Duncan Mill Road, Don Mills, Ontario, Canada M3B 3K9.

This is a work of fiction. Names, characters, places and incidents are either the product of the author's imagination or are used fictitiously, and any resemblance to actual persons, living or dead, business establishments, events or locales is entirely coincidental.

This edition published by arrangement with Harlequin Books S.A.

® and TM are trademarks of the publisher. Trademarks indicated with ® are registered in the United States Patent and Trademark Office, the Canadian Trade Marks Office and in other countries.

www.eHarlequin.com

Printed in U.S.A.

MICHELE DUNAWAY

In first grade Michele Dunaway knew she wanted to be a teacher when she grew up, and by second grade she wanted to be an author. By third grade she was determined to be both, and before her high school class reunion, she succeeded. In addition to writing romance, Michele is a nationally recognized journalism educator who sponsors the yearbook and newspaper at the school where she teaches.

Born and raised in St. Louis (hometown of several NASCAR drivers), Michele has traveled extensively, with the cities and places she's visited often becoming settings for her stories. Described as a woman who does too much but doesn't know how to stop, Michele gardens five acres in her spare time and shares her Missouri River townhome with two young daughters, five lazy house cats and one crazy kitten. Michele loves to hear from readers. You can reach her through her Web site at www.micheledunaway.com.

For Private Peter Waggoner. Thanks for keeping our country safe. While there's no Army guy, this one's for you.

REARVIEW MIRROR:

The beleaguered Branch family is once again the topic of water-cooler conversation as rumors abound about what juicy family secrets will be exposed in the tell-all book written by patriarch Hilton Branch's longtime mistress. No word on how this will affect the careers of NASCAR drivers Bart and Will Branch. Winning now is more important than ever to the twin brothers, if the family is to recover its reputation and financial stability.

CHAPTER ONE

THERE WAS ONLY ONE thing Terri Whalen loved more than stock car racing and even chocolate.

Her truck.

Growing up, the twenty-eight-year-old personal trainer had never been into girls' toys. Her first car had been a small used compact, and she'd saved until she could afford exactly what she wanted. Something big, brash and bold.

The pickup truck she currently drove was an admitted monster that made even the most testosterone-enhanced man green with envy.

First, the diesel-dual crew cab could tow just about anything, including a race car trailer. While most NASCAR Sprint Cup Series race shops hauled their stock cars and backups to the races using eighteen-wheeler transporters, for around town a smaller trailer sufficed and Terri's truck easily got the job done.

Second, the truck was totally tricked out with everything from a custom paint job to custom headers and custom exhaust. Not only could her beast tow, it could also go fast and leave a quarter-mile strip of rubber as it moved from zero to sixty.

Terri bit her lip. At the moment she was worried—and it wasn't about the trip down the church aisle she was about to take. When she'd arrived at the church, the only parking space she'd been able to find had been wedged between a wall and a Dumpster. Not an acceptable choice.

Terri admitted to going overboard about her truck. It was her baby. She washed and waxed the vehicle weekly, more if weather conditions made the paint excessively dirty. She assessed the clear coat daily for any scratches that might mar the finish. She—

"Stop worrying," her friend Pam commanded, and Terri jolted. Pam's comment, however, wasn't directed at Terri, but at Libby, who on her wedding day, had turned into a basket case.

Libby's wedding-day jitters weren't caused by anything inside the sanctuary. The wedding was occurring at a lovely church in downtown Charlotte. The florist had created the most gorgeous floral arrangements in the entire world. Guests had arrived and packed the pews.

The bridesmaids' dresses weren't hideous—they were a shade of lavender that complimented everyone's skin tone. All the bridesmaids had arrived on time and Terri's shoulder-length reddish-brown hair was high in an updo. The groom was there—as were his groomsmen—and everyone was sober. No one's parents had started yelling at each other and everyone seemed to be getting along. The organist charmed the crowd and the air-conditioning cooled.

Terri had been at weddings before where everything that could have gone wrong had. Grooms had shown up drunk, parents had brawled and the sanctuary had been so hot that the bride had passed out during the kiss, hitting her forehead on her husband's chin on the way down.

No, Libby's issue was that, outside the church, someone had forgotten to tell the bride that part of the church parking lot would be getting a fresh coat of asphalt. That paving job was the reason parking was so limited, and why Terri's truck was parked so precariously.

Terri wasn't opposed to parking far away and walking a little, only there hadn't been anywhere close enough not to ruin her hair and makeup or hurt her feet. Already she dreaded tottering down the aisle on the three-inch heels Libby had chosen. Terri usually wore flats.

"Who schedules asphalt paving on a Saturday?" Libby wailed as the acrid smell of molten tar wafted through every crevice and air-conditioning vent, overpowering the floral fragrance.

"Shh, it's fine," Pam soothed. "I checked and the church is packed with your guests. You're gorgeous. Stop stressing. You'll ruin your makeup, and you don't want that."

Libby sniffed once and took the tissue Pam handed her. She dabbed her eyes lightly.

Pam, Terri and Libby had been friends since grade one, even though they were very different. Libby had been the pretty cheerleader, Terri had been the jock, and Pam had been the brain. Together they'd survived four years of high school by sticking together through thick and thin.

Pam looked pointedly at Terri, urging her to say something.

"It'll be great," Terri said, trying to keep Libby's mood upbeat. Today was supposed to be the happiest day of her life. "The ceremony starts in five minutes. It'll be over in twenty. Then we'll all leave for the reception."

"We still have to take pictures," Libby reminded them. Even though she was living with her fiancé, she hadn't wanted him to see her the day of wedding until she walked down the aisle. "And I can't have my receiving line outside while they're dumping tar."

She appeared about ready to burst into tears, so Terri replied quickly, "So have it at the reception. That way you can get the photos done faster and get out of here. The minister can announce the change right before he introduces you."

"That could work." Libby cheered up and Terri gave herself a mental pat on the back for her idea. See? Pam wasn't the only one in the group with smarts. Pam shot Terri a relieved smile, and at that moment the wedding co-ordinator arrived and told them it was time to get started.

The ceremony went without a hitch, if one discounted the occasional clang of dump trucks unloading asphalt that intermingled with the "I do's."

When not concentrating on her official duties, Terri kept her eye on an attractive groomsman directly across the way. He had curly dark hair, smooth olive-toned skin and deep-brown eyes. She'd heard from Libby that Anthony had arrived alone from where he lived in L.A. Better still, he wasn't gay.

He'd also been somewhat slotted into the role of her date, as he was the guy who'd escorted her down the aisle. Both were single. So who knew? A little wedding magic might rub off, and if he felt scrumptious when they danced together…maybe the night and their acquaintanceship would turn into something more.

"Pictures!" the wedding coordinator called, clapping her hands and moving everyone into place. The wedding party posed, girls in front, boys behind, and Terri swore she felt Anthony's hand lightly brush her backside.

"Sorry," he murmured, leaning down to whisper in her ear.

The family photos happened next, and then came a few other shots that included Terri, and finally she and Pam and the other bridesmaids were free to retrieve their belongings and head to the reception. The bride and groom had rented a limo, but everyone else would travel to the banquet hall in their own vehicles.

Now that the church parking lot had emptied of wedding guests, the asphalt company had moved their barriers and started paving over the remaining portions of the lot. Thus, the drivable portion had shrunk in size.

She felt a presence behind her. "Are you driving?" Anthony asked as he came around her right side. "If so, can I catch a ride with you?"

Pam, who'd overheard his question, shot Terri an "ooh" look, giggled and moved past them as she made her way to her car.

"Yeah, I'd be happy to take you," Terri said.

Anthony gave her a killer smile. "Then I'll go get my things."

"I'll start my truck," Terri told him.

Somehow maintaining her balance on the high heels, she made her way down the church steps and headed for where she'd parked.

Hers was the last vehicle in the lot near the portion the company was beginning to pave, and the dump truck made a beep-beep-beep as it backed up into a space ten feet away from her truck.

She'd be able to get out safely; the dump truck was on the other side of those bright orange cones and she had a plenty of room to squeeze through. She walked a little farther, staying on the sidewalk, and then froze when the loud ruckus started. Asphalt crew members yelled, shouted and pointed.

The only explanation for what happened next was that the driver of the dump truck mistook the gas pedal for the brake. Her grandmother had done that once, and ended up driving backward in a circle until she'd crashed into her front porch, totaling both the car and the porch. Luckily her grandmother had been unscathed, albeit a little shaken by the experience.

Even after a nail-biter of a NASCAR race finish, Terri had never understood the expression *Time stands still,* but she understood it now. The driver had somehow lost control. The dump truck careened backward through the cones and orange tape and slammed into the passenger side of her truck.

After the impact, the driver panicked—he kept crushing her vehicle, pushing it until the driver's side hit the wall and the Dumpster. Shouts mixed with crushing sheet metal. Terri winced, somehow too frozen in disbelief to move.

And it wasn't over yet. The back end of the dump truck began to rise, and before anyone could stop it, the gate opened and molten asphalt poured out and washed over her precious baby and onto the parking lot he was supposed to pave.

"What's going on?" Anthony had reached her side, a small carry-on bag in his hand. Terri tried to make her feet move, but she couldn't. Instead, she glanced around, waiting for someone with a camera to come running and tell her this was all fake, perhaps a movie shoot.

But of course it wasn't. She could tell this was reality by the way the paving crew gathered around, screaming at each other. Some stared at her truck. One was on his cell phone. A few others were talking to the driver of the dump truck and helping him down. He appeared shaken and disoriented.

Terri found herself trembling as a big black glob of hot wet asphalt rolled off her truck and hit the pavement with a resounding splat. Her beautiful truck that she always kept so pristine looked as if she'd gone mudding, except for the fact that underneath the hot asphalt the paint bubbled and peeled.

He'd killed her truck.

"Whoever owns that truck isn't going to be too happy," Anthony said. Together they gazed at the unbelievable sight just across the parking lot.

Terri finally found her voice and her feet. "I own it," she told him, taking a step forward.

"Bummer. Well, I'm sure they have insurance. And it's only a truck," Anthony consoled.

He didn't appear too concerned about her loss, and Terri stopped and stared at him. His words were like someone slapping your sunburn. Painful and insensitive.

"I put the pinstripes on myself," she told him, her voice notching upward, trace hints of impending hysteria evident. "It's not just a truck. It was *my* truck."

He held up his hands in a defensive gesture. "Hey, calm down. I'm sure the asphalt company's got insurance. They have to in order to bid on a job like this. It'll get fixed. So relax. Keep things in perspective."

Terri assessed the guy she'd thought had been so handsome and sexy only ten minutes earlier. The wedding magic had already fizzled; the veil was off. To be so cavalier in the face of catastrophe meant only one thing.

He was not the guy for her.

She planted her hands on her hips and sighed at the inevitable. "You know what? I think you better go find another ride."

CHAPTER TWO

TUESDAY AFTERNOON the phone on Max Harper's desk beeped, indicating he had an incoming call on line one. He glanced briefly at his desk calendar. For the entire month of July he'd been positioned in the Claims Department of Rocksolid Insurance Company, working with the supervisors overseeing the insurance adjusters and claim processors. He lifted the receiver. "Max Harper."

"I need a supervisor," the female voice on the other line said without delay. "I have a woman who's demanding to speak with one." The customer-service employee sounded a bit flustered, as if the caller she was dealing with hadn't been all that pleasant.

Although technically Max wasn't a supervisor and the job was beneath his company stature, he hadn't yet fielded an actual customer call. He'd heard tapes and had book knowledge, but that was it. He could use the hands-on experience.

As part of Rocksolid Insurance Company's Rising Stars Program, Max had spent the past seven months being moved about the company and working in various capacities. Having personal experience with an actual customer complaint could only be beneficial.

"What seems to be the problem?" Max asked, ready to tackle the challenge. He'd never been the type of guy to back away from one.

"We're at fault and she's unhappy with the insurance adjuster's decision."

"Is the adjuster available?" Max asked.

"No, he's off today, which is why she's demanding to speak with someone else. The adjuster has declared her truck unable to be repaired and Rocksolid will pay her for its current value. But, she doesn't want the money. She wants the vehicle repaired."

Max leaned back and contemplated that one. Usually the scenario was the other way around. Most people wanted their vehicle declared totaled; they didn't want to drive something that had seen the inside of a body shop and been fixed. They wanted the money so they could go buy something new.

Interested, Max said, "Transfer her file and the call."

As THE SECOND HAND on her watch completed another revolution and the minute hand moved to the ten, indicating that four minutes had passed since she'd been put on hold, Terri tried to keep the steam from blowing out her ears.

The past few days had been a nightmare. She'd missed a good part of the wedding reception because of the damage done to her truck. The police had arrived, taken statements and written a report. Her mom had already been at the banquet hall, and she'd had to leave the reception and return to the church to pick up Terri.

The asphalt company was clearly at fault, so before

she'd eaten a slice of wedding cake, Terri had called their insurance company's 1-800 number and filed a complaint.

When that part was done, the girl inputting the information had told Terri that nothing would happen until Monday. However, Terri could rent a car at her own expense and then be reimbursed. Since her father, crew chief for Bart Branch, was out of town at the NASCAR Sprint Cup Series race at Indianapolis, Terri had borrowed his.

Now it was Tuesday. Fault had been officially determined. She could now rent a car at *their* expense, up to twenty dollars a day. That meant she'd be driving some midget economy car that her truck would have eaten for breakfast.

Terri tapped her fingers on the arm of the chair. The moment she'd heard the insurance company's decision, she'd asked for a supervisor. She'd learned that those were the people who could get things done.

"Ms. Whalen?" the customer-service rep was back on the line.

"Yes?"

"I'm going to transfer you now. Thank you for calling Rocksolid Insurance Company."

Within seconds the woman was gone, but this time Terri didn't hear any annoying hold music. Instead, she heard a few clicks and then an extremely deep voice said, "This is Max Harper. How may I help you?"

Terri jolted a little. His voice was rich and full. He could easily be a voice-over announcer, instead of some guy working behind a desk at an insurance company. She hesitated, a tad rattled by his tone.

"Ms. Whalen?" he prompted.

"I'm here," she replied, regaining her composure. This was about her truck, not some faceless stranger at the other end of the connection who had a voice like velvet.

"I understand you have some questions about the settlement offer," Max Harper said.

"I do," Terri replied, her ire beginning to build again. Normally she was a calm, reasonable person. When it came to her truck, however, she became a bit high-strung and emotional. It wasn't just *any* truck, and the whole situation was unfathomable and extremely unfair. Her truck had been safely parked, for goodness' sake!

"I want my truck repaired. I don't want it declared a write-off," she said, getting straight to the point.

"I have your case file, including pictures, in front of me. It's a custom truck?"

Terri attempted to remain calm. "Yes. Do you know how much work I put into that truck? Using my own two hands?"

"That's the problem," Max admitted. "You should be receiving a detailed breakdown of our decision in the mail tomorrow, but in this particular case, you are over the eighty-percent cost. We estimate we will have to pay almost ninety-five percent of your current vehicle's value to bring it back to its former condition. Therefore, as the repair estimate is over the eighty-percent threshold, we declare the vehicle a loss and pay you for its value."

"I can't even *buy* that particular truck model anymore," Terri protested, shaking slightly. She gripped the phone tighter. "It's a limited-edition model. They only made that version for one year as a special promotion geared for NASCAR race fans."

"I can understand your frustration," Max soothed.

"I doubt it," she shot back. "I built most of that truck myself. My father and I spent hours together on it."

"Which is another reason for our decision. You also had an inordinate number of custom parts manufactured specifically for your vehicle. You did the work yourself, meaning the labor wasn't even factored in. However, that's something we must do when making our decision. As I said, company policy is that we declare a vehicle a total loss when repairing it will cost more than eighty percent of what the vehicle is currently worth. I'm sorry."

"You cannot base my truck's value on some stupid policy," Terri said, trying to keep from shouting. "It's worth a lot more than you think. I have receipts for all the parts. I just installed a new stereo/DVD system. Was that damaged? Did you pay me at one hundred percent for that? It's not even a week old."

She took a breath and attempted to release her frustration. This was ridiculous.

"I will be happy to look at any additional documentation you have," Max intoned, and Terri pictured some stodgy supervisor in a suit sitting in a windowless cubicle. All he wanted to do was stamp Case Closed on her file. He didn't care about her, just his company's bottom line.

When she'd first been connected, she'd heard the recording saying that their conversation "might be recorded for quality purposes." Basically that meant the insurance company was trying to cover its rear end. The recording would magically disappear if it was incriminating, but would definitely be pulled out if it benefited the company later down the road. She shook her head in disgust.

Her case wasn't big enough to sue over. Although she would, Terri told herself, hoping her determination wasn't just bravado. She was like David up against Goliath. Just because no one was injured didn't mean they could have their way at her expense.

"Give me a number where I can fax you," she demanded. "And I want to see my truck. I want to see for myself what can be salvaged."

"Once we settle, the truck belongs to us," Max replied.

Terri forced herself to relax her grip on the receiver. She'd clutched it so hard her knuckles had whitened. She also counted her lucky stars that her uncle was an insurance agent. Terri knew how the system worked. She wasn't some in-the-dark consumer that companies could take advantage of.

"Yes, but I have the legal right to assess the damage myself and call in my own expert for an estimate. This is one hundred percent your client's fault. I am the victim here. You will not take shortcuts with me."

She thought she heard him chuckle. Then again, maybe the noise was simply a trick of her ears, for he started telling her his contact information and Terri scrambled to jot it all down. She'd been prepared with a piece of paper and a pen, but he spoke quickly. She read his phone and fax numbers back to him to make certain she had both correct.

"Let's talk at the end of the week," Max said. "Is this the number I can call you at, or is this one—" he rattled off her cell phone number "—better?"

"The second, my cell, is best," Terri told him. She disconnected and set her office phone aside. No matter what, temporarily she was going to have to find another truck. She glanced at the calendar hanging on the wall, hardly believing that August was only a few days away. Her cell phone trilled again, and Terri glanced at the number before answering. "Terri Whalen."

"Hi, Terri, Bonds here. I have a job for you."

Bonds was Ricky Bondoni, Terri's agent. He preferred to be known just as Bonds, making him sound more 007ish.

"Let's hear it," Terri said, thinking she could use some good news. The last time he'd called, she'd found herself in sunny California a few days later shooting a commercial for a beer company. All she'd had to do was suit up in a stock car driver's uniform, pretend to be the man and drive his car around a few city streets. She'd made some pretty nice chump change for the stunt work and gotten a vacation at the same time.

Terri was a card-carrying member of the Screen Actors Guild even though no one ever saw her. It was a little-known fact that race car drivers didn't actually do any of their own driving in the commercials—they only filmed the parts where the camera saw their face.

She'd gotten started in commercials while she was racing in the NASCAR Craftsman Truck Series. She'd made more than fifteen commercial appearances since—one even included her driving while waving a chicken drumstick out the window.

"This job's actually in your backyard," Bonds said.

"No travel?" Terri said, disappointed. Charlotte, North Carolina, was baking under the summer heat. A vacation somewhere cooler would have been ideal.

Bonds laughed. "Nope. The company headquarters for the commercial you'll be shooting is in Charlotte and they've arranged to rent the track there. You'll basically be doing what you do best, pretending to race."

"Ha, you're so funny," she said. So she hadn't made a career out of racing trucks. She'd at least tried. "How much am I getting? Did I tell you my truck got totaled? I'm still fighting with the insurance company, but with the amount of damage I saw, even if it gets repaired I'm going to have to start over."

Bonds whistled. "That'll be pricey. You e-mailed me a picture of your monstrosity." He then named the figure Terri would be paid.

She was pleased with the amount. "That sounds good. Much more than the last few times."

"Yep. I was able to get you a little more money since you're the star and you don't have to travel. Aside from a lap or two racing, you have to drive down pit road while they film a pit stop."

"That doesn't sound too hard," Terri said, knowing the production of any commercial wasn't simple. For the drumstick deal, the director had had her wave the chicken leg five different ways, recording each take. When the final commercial had aired, they'd used the first one they'd filmed.

"It's a one-day job. Thursday," Bonds told her.

"Two days from now?" That was pretty fast. Usually Terri was hired a few weeks in advance, especially if she had to make travel arrangements.

"They just got all the details finalized. Something about having some creative differences with the advertising firm they'd hired. Anyway, everything's settled and they want to air the commercials during the Chase for the NASCAR Sprint Cup. So clear your schedule if you want the job," Bonds said.

Filming gave Terri the opportunity to be behind the wheel of a stock car. "I'll take it. You know me."

"I do, which is why I love you. I'm faxing the contract at this very moment," Bonds said, and Terri envisioned him pressing a button. "You should have it within seconds. I'm also sending the details of the shoot—times, locations, those sorts of things."

In the background, Terri's fax machine began to whir, signaling the arrival of her contract. She stood, stretching a little. "They're here," she told Bonds once she'd checked the machine.

"Great. Sign those and get them back to me within the hour."

"I can do that. Hold on. Let me just read it quickly before I hang up." Terri began skimming the contract and then she paused. He had to be kidding. "Hey, Bonds? Are you sure you couldn't have gotten me even more money?"

"Is something wrong?" He sounded worried.

No, nothing was wrong. It was more a case of fate being ironic. Terri grimaced. "No, no. I'm doing the commercial. Don't panic. But can I crash one of the cars while I'm at it?"

"You have to be joking." She could hear his horror and laughed as she pictured Bonds's apoplectic face. "That's why you get all the gigs. You're that good. You don't wreck," he said. "Wrecking costs money."

"Yeah, but a little payback might be nice. You do see the client's name, don't you?"

"Yeah. The Rocksolid Insurance Company. They sponsor Billy Budd."

Terri gave a deep sigh. Life wasn't fair. "You're lucky I'm a professional, Bonds. Always remember that."

"Why?"

"Because Rocksolid's the insurance company representing the asphalt company that wrecked my truck."

CHAPTER THREE

"So we're going to be on a movie set?"

"Not exactly," Max told his twelve-year-old daughter, Mandy, as he drove through the tunnel toward the infield area of the race track. "Rocksolid is making a commercial today."

"Oh. So we won't see any movie stars? Just some drivers?" Mandy asked.

"No movie stars," Max told her, glancing at his watch as he followed the signs to where he was to park. "You might get to meet Billy Budd. He'll be here at one."

Max had learned long ago to talk straight with his daughter. She'd turn thirteen in September, which meant she was entering eighth grade once school resumed in the fall. She took all challenge classes and participated in the school's gifted program.

"I guess Billy's okay. Lynn thinks he's hot. I wish she could have come." Lynn was Mandy's best friend. The two were thicker than thieves and had been for three years. Mandy glanced at the radio, reading the clock. "It's only noon."

Max nodded. "Right. We have an hour before Billy shows."

Once August arrived—tomorrow—Max would be transferred out of the Claims Department and into Rocksolid's PR department. But his first task began today, overseeing a commercial shoot. Nothing like being immediately tossed into the fray.

"The director has been filming since eight, but we weren't due until now. We're meeting Mr. Henson and his daughter for lunch. You met them at the company picnic last June."

"I remember. His daughter's nice."

"So what's bugging you, then?" Max asked as he parked. His four-door car was nothing special, but he kept the newer-model sedan immaculate in case he ever had to ferry business associates.

"Mom says NASCAR drivers aren't famous," Mandy said. She drew a breath, as if weighing how much trouble she'd be in if she said what was on her mind next.

"Spit it out," Max said. Personally he loved NASCAR, but his ex-wife didn't share his enthusiasm for the sport.

"Mom also says that this isn't a real set. I told her you were taking me and she wasn't very impressed. Lynn was, though."

Max checked his rising temper. Lola, with her dreams of becoming a famous actress, had several times set out for Tinsel Town but so far failed to take Hollywood by storm.

Actually she'd only managed a few film roles as an extra, but her agent kept promising she was only days away from her big break. Of course those days had turned into years, so Max wasn't holding his breath. It was always the same old story and Lola had bounced back and forth between California and North Carolina ever since she'd divorced Max and left him and two-year-old Mandy behind.

"This is a real set," Max told his daughter. "Commercials are just as important as movies. They might be even harder to produce. How long's a movie?"

"An hour and a half? Maybe two?" Mandy said.

"Exactly. That's a long time. This commercial will only last thirty seconds. It's got to grab the viewer and make him think insurance, specifically Rocksolid Insurance."

"I guess commercials do get forgotten pretty quickly."

"And they don't get new lives on DVD, either."

She laughed. "True. I hate commercials at the start of DVDs."

"Well, today Rocksolid is actually shooting three different commercials. The other two are even shorter. One's fifteen seconds and the other's ten. They'll film everything they need at one time and put it all together in editing."

Mandy seemed a bit more impressed as she said, "Ten seconds is short."

"Yes, which is why every second counts. This project's been in the works for over six months."

"I didn't know it was so detailed."

"Yep."

Max exhaled some of his tension as Mandy relaxed. He also made a mental note to speak with Lola. Parenting wasn't a competition. His ex didn't need to cast negative aspersions on Max or his job and thus destroy Mandy's enjoyment of a day like today.

"Maybe you can get Billy's autograph for Lynn," Max said.

"That would be cool," Mandy replied. "She'd like that."

Max opened his door and Mandy did the same. "Ready?"

She nodded.

"Then let's do this."

THERE WAS NOTHING Terri loved to do more than race. Too bad she'd been so bad at it.

She didn't have that innate instinct that *made* a driver. She wasn't one who could see the wind or who somehow sensed when a space to slide through would open up. To be a champion was more than training. You had to have the gift and the burning hunger. You had to eat, breathe and sleep racing, forsaking everything else.

She'd enjoyed her tenure in the NASCAR Craftsman Truck Series, but in points she'd lived somewhere around twenty-eighth.

While it wasn't at the bottom of the pack, it wasn't where she'd envisioned herself, either. The highest finish she'd ever had was at Texas. She'd placed fifteenth. The series was often a stepping-stone, but for Terri there would be no climb out of trucks and into a NASCAR Nationwide Series car.

Her tenure had proved one thing—that she didn't have the gift and couldn't learn to compensate.

But Terri was stubborn, so she'd revised her game plan and settled for the next-best thing, which was still being in the car, either doing testing for her dad or, on days like today when she filmed a commercial, racing at the same high speeds the NASCAR Sprint Cup Series drivers ran.

"Okay, now as you come around Turn Four, I want you to be at least five feet out in front. This time have a gap between you and the pack." The radio in her helmet broadcast the director's instructions.

"Got it," Terri radioed back. The last time around he'd wanted the cars behind her to be on her bumper. The other stunt drivers got their instructions and fell back the requisite distance. She zoomed down the front stretch, crossed the finish line, and then heard the director shout, "Cut! Bring it in!"

Adrenaline filled Terri as she slowed the car, taking it on its "victory lap" and then driving down pit road. The others followed; it was lunchtime.

Terri parked, removed her helmet and unhooked herself from the HANS device. She slid from the car and gave a high five to one of her "crew" members. She'd worked with him on two of her previous commercials.

"Great job, Terri," one of the other stunt drivers said, exiting his car.

"Thanks, Mark," she said.

"Heck, you drive better than Billy himself," someone else joked, and as a group, those who'd driven the cars walked over to the tables to eat.

"Hey, speaking of Billy, there he is with the brass," Mark said. "Thought he wasn't coming until later."

Terri glanced over. Billy Budd stood next to two men wearing polo shirts and Dockers pants. Everyone else was dressed in jeans and T-shirts, including Billy, who wore a T-shirt advertising his sponsor Rocksolid. "Those must be the company guys."

"Yeah, and it must be 'take your daughter to work' day," Mark snickered, and Terri saw two girls sitting at a table. One listened to music and the other played a handheld gaming device. Both had earbuds in their ears and half-eaten plates of food in front of them.

"They look bored," the guy walking next to Terri said. He'd flown in from California and did stunt driving for several television police shows. They'd met that morning, but she'd blanked on his name.

"Just a little bit," Terri agreed. "Save me a seat and I'll see you guys in a minute." She walked off, making a beeline for the restroom.

She was washing her hands when one of the two girls came in. The girl with the game device, Terri recalled. The girl listening to music had blond hair. This girl had curly black hair, pale skin and a pixie mouth.

Her dark-blue eyes fixed on Terri. "I didn't think girls drove race cars."

"You didn't, huh?" Terri replied, having grown accustomed to people saying that when she raced trucks.

"Are you any good?" the girl asked.

Terri laughed. She'd long ago stopped focusing on her shortcomings. "If I was, I wouldn't be here. Nope, I got as far as the truck series. I'm a stunt driver. I'm playing Billy Budd."

"My mom's an actress."

"I guess in a way I am, too." Terri grabbed a paper towel and started drying her hands.

"Been in anything famous?" the girl persisted.

"Fifteen commercials and a few racing movies."

"Like?"

Terri named the movies and the girl's eyes widened.

"I saw that last one. I love…" Excitedly the girl named the actor who'd played the lead role.

"Who doesn't like him?" Terri agreed. The guy was steaming. Too bad he had a wife and five kids.

Then again, all the good guys were either happily married or gay. The single ones had too many issues and the divorced ones came with far too much baggage.

"Catch you later," Terri told the girl. She tossed the paper towel in the trash and strode from the restroom. Her stomach growled, and concentrating on the buffet, she narrowly avoided bumping into a man who'd walked up at the same time.

"Sorry," she mumbled, glancing at him. She pegged him at two inches taller than Bart Branch, making the guy six-four. He probably weighed around 225 pounds, but he wasn't fat. Instead, he had broad shoulders and a wide chest, which tapered down to narrow hips and long legs. Yeah, he certainly fit the description tall, dark and handsome, with that black hair and those dark-blue eyes.

"Is my daughter in there?" he asked.

His voice startled her. It seemed familiar somehow. She reminded herself that he worked for the company she currently hated and the one she was driving for. He was also a family man, and she avoided those types. "Girl about twelve? Yes."

"Thanks," he said, not really moving out of her way.

Instead, he assessed her, and Terri couldn't help it, she bristled. "Yes, like your daughter asked, women do drive race cars. And I'm portraying Billy Budd. I'm his stunt double. Now if you'd excuse me…"

He reached forward, lightly touched her forearm. The skin there prickled and the hair stood up. She'd left her uniform unzipped and unfolded at her waist. "Have we met?" he asked.

So he found her familiar, too, but if she'd met this man she would have remembered. He wasn't the kind you forgot.

"I don't think so," she said. "I'm just your driver. I don't use your company for insurance."

"Have you ever gotten a quote? We're usually the best deal in town and our coverage is rock solid."

"A clever slogan, but I'm not interested. I'm already dealing with a claim against your company, and I'm not really too pleased with your service."

He arched an eyebrow. Damn, but this guy was handsome. "No?"

"Not at all," Terri said, sensing the invisible current humming between them. Strange that he would affect her like this.

"Terri, you're wasting time." Mark yelled from where he was sitting and eating. "Get moving, girl, or you won't get anything to eat."

Terri gave the man a smile that didn't quite meet her eyes. Something about him disturbed her, and she didn't like the feeling.

"Sorry to cut this short, but I'm due back on set in twenty minutes," she told him, grateful for the interruption. "I need to have lunch or I'll be starving the rest of the day."

"Yeah, sure. Sorry," the man replied. As she moved closer to the buffet, she glanced back over her shoulder, seeing him waiting there for his daughter. He definitely was a prime specimen. A man with a kid, however, was not a complication she needed.

HER NAME WAS Terri. No, it couldn't be. What were the odds he'd run into her here? Max waited for Mandy to exit the restroom and then he strode back to where Alan Henson waited with Billy Budd. Billy's own PR person had joined them, and Billy was autographing a few items for the growing crowd, including Mandy.

"Who's that?" Max asked Billy a few minutes later when the crowd thinned. "Do you know her?"

Billy scanned the crowd. "Who?"

"Your stunt double," Max said easily. "She's at that table over there."

"Oh, yeah. I know her," Billy said. He greeted a few more people, signed a few more autographs before he could finish explaining. "I used to race with her a few years back. That's Terri Whalen. She's Philip Whalen's daughter—he's Bart Branch's crew chief. You heard of Bart? Races for PDQ? The one with the philandering father who's involved in that embezzlement scandal?"

Max had heard of the scandal. It had been all over the news media since February. "Terri Whalen."

"Yeah," Billy said, shrugging. "She dropped off the circuit a while back but still keeps her foot in the door by doing this kind of stuff."

Max watched as Terri lifted a forkful of salad to her

mouth. The woman on the other end of the phone, the claimant against Rocksolid.

He'd pictured some big brute, a Neanderthal type, a woman with too much testosterone.

He'd certainly been way off. The slim woman sitting with the other stunt drivers was a vision of femininity. Sure, she had some tomboy in her, but his daughter had that. And from the tight T-shirt she wore, Max could tell Terri had curves. She smiled, and it tugged at something deep inside him.

He'd gotten his first impression of her over the phone when she'd been royally ticked off at his adjuster's decision. Now he had a fuller picture of her and found himself in a conundrum.

Fact was, he had to call her tomorrow to discuss the results of his review of her case file. She wasn't going to be pleased. He didn't even want to *think* about how she would react. He already knew.

The director approached, greeted Alan Henson and Max and then asked Billy to join him for some last-minute instructions. Billy turned to Max. "Gotta go. You want me to introduce you to Terri or something?"

Max shook his head. Tomorrow would indeed be interesting. "No, it's fine," Max told Billy. "We've already met."

CHAPTER FOUR

THIS WAS THE SECOND weekend Terri wasn't going to be at the race track to fulfill her duties as a fitness trainer, but she needed to get the situation with her truck settled. Her NASCAR clients understood and promised to follow Terri's exercise regime on their own.

This morning she'd received a call from a Rocksolid secretary asking her if she could meet Max Harper that afternoon at the salvage yard where her vehicle had been towed. After shuffling a couple of appointments, Terri was on her way.

At least he was *meeting* with her, instead of handling this over the phone. Even better, one of her dad's best buddies owned the yard. She'd known Joe since she was four and driving her first go-cart. He'd at least be honest about the status of her truck.

The salvage yard was in the outskirts of Mooresville, and the pathetic little rental whined as she tried to make it go at least the speed limit; it was largely useless on rural roads.

Unlike her beloved truck. She'd done some online searching last night after her workout, but nothing out there on the market appealed to her in the slightest.

The idea of buying another truck and starting over from scratch horrified her. She'd planned on having her truck for another few years. Diesel engines lasted forever if they were maintained properly. She'd envisioned her truck being one of those customized classics someday—something her grandchildren could admire.

She put on her blinker, letting the huge pickup hovering behind her know she would soon be out of his way. She turned onto the smaller asphalt road leading to Joe's. By the time she'd gone half a mile, the asphalt had changed to gravel and the car bumped along until she'd reached the beat-up red mailbox labeled Joe's Auto Salvage.

Terri turned in the driveway, and within a few feet the trees surrounding the property disappeared, and row after row of junked cars took their place. Joe had over twenty acres of salvage, and he'd moved into the twenty-first century by having every auto on his property cataloged and entered in a computer database.

She found the parking area in front of the trailer that served as the office, and stepped out. An old hound dog raised his head, got to his feet, and lumbered down the steps of the small porch to check her out.

"Don't mind Rex," a voice called, and then Joe himself came around the corner. He was wiping his hands on a rag, and he stopped short when he saw her. "Terri!"

"Hey, Joe. I hear you got my truck." She gave him a smile.

"Girl, that thing's a wreck. I hope they paid you well." Joe gave the dog's head a quick pat and then crossed to Terri. "Tell me it wasn't your fault."

"No. Some asphalt truck backed into it."

"You got tar all over, and the paint's peeled even where it ain't covered."

"They want to declare it a total loss," Terri said, hating the quiver that crept into her voice. She'd promised herself she wouldn't get emotional today.

Joe shook his head, and the dog, seeing he wasn't getting any further attention, returned to the porch and resumed his nap. "It's trashed. They even punctured one of your tires. The only things worth saving are some of the engine parts."

"So you think they did the right thing by scrapping it?" she asked.

"Do you have the time to redo it?" Joe asked.

"Of course I do!" Terri protested immediately.

Joe widened his stance. "Does your dad? Your mama been on him to retire."

Terri sighed. Some of her best memories were of working with her father on the truck. But now that he was Bart's crew chief, her dad didn't have the time. His last driver had had such natural talent that he'd been a winner from the get-go. Bart took a lot more nurturing and a lot more of Philip's time. Bart had the innate ability, but he hadn't yet harnessed the full power of his gift.

"My dad's got his hands full," Terri admitted.

"Then take their money and go buy something else. What are they offering you?"

Terri named the new figure the secretary had recited today. "I faxed them a bunch of my receipts. It's five thousand higher than their last offer."

Joe laughed. "That's good. Take them for all you

can." He looked up. "Figured the insurance-company guy was going to get lost once or twice comin' here, but I think that's him."

A four-door sedan came crunching down the gravel driveway. The dog raised his head and let out a howl. "Hush there," Joe admonished, and the dog put his head on his paws. "Old Rex here's not used to company this time of day. We only operate by appointment and don't usually see people in the afternoon. I'm kinda semiretired. Maybe thinkin' of selling someday."

"Well, thank you for seeing me."

"Girl, you're welcome anytime." Joe scratched the top of his bald head and waited while the Rocksolid representative climbed out. The man's suit jacket flapped about his waist as he reached inside the car and grabbed his briefcase.

Joe put two thumbs under his overall straps and Terri shifted her weight and tilted her head to the side. He wore sunglasses, but she recognized him as the guy from the track yesterday. While they hadn't spoken again after their encounter outside the restroom, she'd sensed him watching her. She wasn't too happy to see him.

"Max Harper?" Joe greeted.

"Yes, sir," Max replied, reaching to shake Joe's hand now that he'd reached them. He turned to Terri. "Ms. Whalen."

"Max," she said, giving herself an edge by greeting him so familiarly. "It's good to see you again."

"You two know each other?" Joe asked.

She gritted her teeth as Max smiled. *The jerk! He'd*

known! "Max was on the set of the commercial I filmed yesterday."

"I do a little of everything for Rocksolid," he said easily, oblivious to her irritation. "I'm finishing up Terri's case as a favor for the Claims Department."

"Ah," Joe said, obviously not understanding a bit and not too concerned about his lack of knowledge. "Shall we go see the truck? I got it parked just behind here."

They followed Joe to the truck. This was the first time Terri had seen the damage in its entirety. She cringed and tried to bite back the tears. She'd seen the passenger side, all mangled and bent from the dump truck's tailgate. But the driver's side was worse. Pushed up against the wall and the metal Dumpster, it was completely caved in. The paint was gone on most of the vehicle, either scraped or boiled off by the tar. Her custom lights atop the truck had melted, the chrome lusterless and deformed.

"I didn't realize it was this bad," Terri said.

"It ain't pretty," Joe said, stating the obvious. He glanced at Max. "You got papers for me?"

Max nodded, his dark hair glinting in the sunlight. "I brought your storage-fee agreement and payment. They're in my car."

"Then I'll leave you to it and you can bring 'em to the office," Joe said, walking away.

Max glanced at Terri. "I am truly sorry this happened."

Terri ignored him and yanked on the rear driver's-side door. It gave a sickening creak but opened.

She stuck her head inside, and then stepped back to let the rancid odor escape. The stench was awful. Even with the best upholstery cleaner, the interior would require a lot of work. Despite her resolve, tears welled in her eyes.

"Are you okay?"

She turned, finding Max mere inches behind her. Since she was five-five, his six-four bulk towered over her by almost a foot. "No, I'm not okay," she said. She fought tears. Pride dictated she not cry. "This was my baby. I did all the work. I put on those lights. I wired the stereo system. I…"

A sob escaped her and within seconds, her whole body shook from the enormity of it all. Her voice choked. "This isn't fair! I don't want another truck. I wanted this one! I put my whole life into this! Why can't your company see that?"

MAX STARED at Terri Whalen. He hated tears. Tears were never good. No matter how tough a guy was, a woman's tears were the one thing that could bring a man to his knees.

"I guess that's why policies are black and white," he said awkwardly, hating the words the moment they came out of his mouth. He'd sounded crass, cold. And his brothers always teased him about being Mr. Sensitivity. Not in *this* case.

"This is so not right!" Terri's nose and face had reddened. "Your client ruined my truck. Please. I just want my truck. Not some new one. My dad and I spent hours doing this. The time together brought us closer. Don't you understand?"

Actually, Max did. He'd gotten his love of basketball from his father, who'd been the PE teacher at his high school and the team coach. His dad had spent many hours with him working on drills, and that work had paid off when Max received a full scholarship to State University.

He stepped closer, willing Terri to understand *his* position. "This isn't personal. It's business."

"I hate that excuse," Terri stated. "Companies hide behind it all the time. Put a human face on the situation for a change. Look at me."

Max looked. He couldn't help himself. She was a spitfire. He'd never met anyone quite like her. She intrigued him. Even enraged, she was beautiful.

"You have to admit it stinks a bit," he said, wrinkling his nose at the asphalt odor that showed no sign of ebbing.

"I'm sure that can be taken care of," Terri said. He watched as she climbed onto the backseat and ran her finger over the ceiling.

He leaned inside. The tar hadn't melted through. She climbed into the front, giving him a great view of her jean-clad backside. Then she slid into the driver's seat and popped the hood. She also ran her fingers over her radio and DVD system.

She pushed on the driver's door, and it didn't budge. Max pulled from the outside and together they got it open. She'd stopped crying, but her face was still red. He noticed she didn't wear makeup. Rivers of black mascara always accompanied his ex's tears.

"You do understand, don't you, that this truck was my lifeblood? It's depressing. And I'm driving around in that little piece of…" She bit off the expletive and Max remembered the subcompact she'd been driving.

"This truck could haul a race trailer," she went on. "That car won't even pull my Jet Ski. Thank God it's only a rental."

"I'm sorry," Max repeated. He felt like a cad, but there was nothing else he could say. The numbers added up to over eighty percent. Heck, even state law was on his side. The process was fairly simple. She'd sign the papers and then Rocksolid would send paperwork to the State of North Carolina declaring the car a loss. The vehicle would be wiped out of the title database and a salvage yard would do the rest, which was simply tearing apart the truck and selling various parts for scrap.

Even though he'd never been in a car accident himself, he sympathized with her. She'd invested time and talent. Nothing could compensate for those. For most people, money made things better. Terri wasn't most people.

He watched as she shook her head sadly, swishing her reddish-brown shoulder-length hair. She began to push on the hood, trying to force it up so she could assess the engine. Max came around and helped, and together they got the warped hood open.

"Why are you doing this?" she demanded, a smear of grime on her right cheekbone. "Isn't it your job to simply sit in your ivory tower and impersonally write out checks? You didn't have to come get your hands dirty."

"I know," he said. "Look, if it helps, be angry with me. Go ahead. I reviewed your case personally and I'm not a supervisor. Those people work for me. But company policy is based on state laws. And we have to follow those to the letter."

"Good for you," Terri shot back. "*Policy*. It's always policy."

"I know I'd be ticked off if something like this happened to a vehicle I loved," he said. "It's obvious you care a great deal for your truck."

"There's no amount of money that can replace the memories of building this or of what I'd planned to do with it in the future," Terri told him sadly, her anger disappearing. "My dad has a 1960 Corvette. It's a classic. This truck was to be the same."

Tears came again and impulsively Max did the first thing that came to mind. Not the most professional thing, but the first thing. He reached out and drew her into his arms.

IT HAD BEEN a while since Terri had had a man's arms around her.

But the fact that these arms belonged to Max Harper had her hiccupping, drying her tears and stepping back.

She'd liked being held by him. He'd smelled divine. His arms had been strong and steady. She'd heard his heart thumping inside his chest.

"Sorry. That was inappropriate," Max said, obviously at as much of a loss as she was. "I apologize."

Terri didn't trust herself to speak, so she simply turned away and glanced at the engine now that the hood was up. Most of the things in the middle appeared undamaged. The front passenger-side components, however, had been crushed by the dump truck.

She climbed onto the bumper and began a closer

inspection. She'd have to do some research. Even if she could salvage some parts, there was no guarantee that any of these custom parts could be made to fit another engine. She jumped off, prepared to ask Joe not to scrap her engine until she'd had a chance to talk to her dad.

She whirled to go find Joe and bumped into Max. This time both her hands pressed against his chest, and he caught her, steadying her. To any onlooker, it probably appeared as if they were dancing and she was preparing to dip!

"We've got to quit bumping into each other like this," Max said, his deep voice catching at the back of his throat.

"Uh…yeah," Terri replied, annoyed with herself for sounding like one of those breathless idiotic women you see in a bad B-grade movie.

She disentangled herself from his arms. "Thank you," she said. "Twice is quite enough."

"I'm not trying to touch you," he stated, backing up a foot. "It's accidental."

"And you're the expert on accidents," Terri replied, irritated that she'd liked his touch. She liked a lot about Max Harper, such as his looks and his voice. Another time and another place, he might be a man she'd want to get to know. Now she wanted him and this whole unfortunate situation behind her. She'd cried in front of him. That was simply unacceptable behavior for her. She was tough, not a pushover. She refused to show him any more weakness.

"I want two thousand more for my truck before I consider signing any settlement papers," she said. "I do believe that's fair and you're still lowballing me with the amount your secretary quoted me earlier today."

His relieved expression made the dimples in his cheeks deepen. "So you'll agree to a settlement?"

"Do I have a choice? I'm tired of your company policies. However, I know what I deserve and I will fight until I get fair compensation for my loss."

"I'll review the paperwork you sent me one more time and let you know."

Terri gave him a tight smile and crossed her arms over her chest. "I'd prefer not to drag this out, but I will if necessary."

He held up his palms in surrender and she noticed a few calluses. He wasn't afraid to use his hands.

"I'll address your claim first thing Monday morning," he said in his defense.

Terri closed the hood and slammed the truck doors shut. Then she walked with Max back to the front of Joe's office.

Joe was waiting for them on the porch and he rose to his feet. "What's the verdict?"

"It got an asphalt bath," Terri told him, her tone resigned. This time she refused to cry, but she still felt moisture in her eyes and a grip on her heart. "I might be able to salvage a few things, but I need to talk to my dad first."

Joe had been right, and he nodded his sympathy.

"It'll be fine," Terri said, biting the inside of her cheek to stop the tears before either man saw them. "I'll just take the money, after all, and start over. When can I get my check? And a decent rental?"

Max cracked a slight smile. "The rental I can arrange today. The check will require the title and your signing the settlement."

Now that she'd decided, she became a woman of action. She wanted the ugliness over with. "Fine. I can get you the title. It's at my house. Why don't you do the review today so we can get this done. Say by five?"

Max glanced at his watch and she peered at hers. "It's already four. The office closes at five. You could come in on Monday and meet with my secretary and—"

"No." She cut him off. "I'm not signing over the title and leaving it with anyone but you."

Max reached into his pocket and removed a cell phone. He checked the calendar function. "I could do Monday afternoon at three. I will call and authorize a larger rental car. You should have something comparable to what you owned. That is our policy."

"It would have been nice if someone had followed that policy a little sooner," Terri said, sarcasm obvious. "The wannabe over there leaves a lot to be desired. It doesn't even have power windows."

"I feel your pain," he replied, equaling her sarcastic tone.

"Your customer service rep didn't," Terri stated flatly.

"I'm no longer involved in that department, but believe me, I will address your issues next week at the management meeting."

He reached into a pocket and drew out a business card. "Call me Monday after ten and we'll go over the settlement statement and see if it's agreeable before you show up at three."

"Fine," Terri said, taking the card and shoving it in the front pocket of her jeans.

Max stood there expectantly. "If there's nothing else…"

Terri was highly cognizant of the fact that Joe was still on the front porch. Oh, he'd put his oversize body into a rocker and tilted his beat-up ball cap down in front of his face, but she had no doubt he was listening to everything. Unlike the dog, Joe was only pretending to sleep.

"No, we're good," Terri said.

"Then I'll speak with you on Monday." With that, Max retrieved some paperwork from his briefcase, gave it to a newly revived Joe, climbed into his car and drove away.

BY SIX THAT EVENING, Max had Mandy ready for her weekend visit with her mother. After he'd arranged for the upgrade of Terri's rental car, he'd retrieved Mandy from camp and left her to her own packing.

By seven-fifteen, Lola was forty-five minutes late. She'd chosen the six-thirty pickup time herself, which made her being late even more annoying.

Max sighed. When she'd been younger, Mandy had waited impatiently for her mother's arrival; she'd constantly looked out the window. As she'd gotten older, she'd learned that such vigilance wasn't rewarded. Nowadays when she visited her mother, Mandy watched television or used the computer until her mother showed up, whenever that happened to be.

Oh, Lola always had an excuse for her tardiness. Sometimes her plane from L.A. was late. A few times she'd had car trouble. Once she'd had to cancel the entire weekend because a job opportunity had come up. Max had long ago stopped questioning the validity of Lola's many excuses.

Like the boy who cried wolf too many times, Lola's reasons began to fall on deaf ears, for the truth was, Mandy was low on Lola's priority list. Her daughter was mainly an accessory to be trotted out when needed. Max wasn't certain what the occasion was this weekend. Lola had been acting a bit strange since she'd returned from L.A.

Oh, he knew Lola loved her daughter in her own way, but he also knew that not all love was for the best.

Heck, even his and Lola's "love" had been mostly lust. They'd been two immature college kids deluding themselves into thinking that what they had would stand the test of time.

They'd met in their senior year, when they were young and fresh and thought they were immortal. An unplanned pregnancy? He'd believed that happened only to irresponsible people—until it had happened to him.

So he'd done the right thing and married Lola, but in the long run, they didn't have what it took to succeed as a couple. Hindsight was always twenty-twenty.

Being a married man with a kid on the way had made Max grow up fast and give up any dream of playing pro basketball. Lola, however, didn't give up her dream. The most important thing in her life was achieving fame as an actress. The most important thing in *his* life was his daughter. She was his world, and he'd lay down his life for her.

Even if it meant protecting her from her own mother.

Max had long ago stopped suggesting Lola make the

biweekly visits she'd fought for during the divorce proceedings. She didn't utilize the weekends the court had granted her, and in his opinion, the less often Lola breezed in and out of his daughter's life, the better off Mandy would be. Mandy needed her mother, yes, but not when her mother treated her as an afterthought. Max and his mother had been the ones to explain the facts of life to Mandy, not Lola.

Max poked his head into the TV room and saw that Mandy was watching some TV show. "You doing okay? Hungry?"

"A little. Has Mom called?" she asked.

"No," Max said.

Mandy rolled her eyes and sighed. She was used to this and far too cynical for a twelve-year-old. "What are you doing for dinner?"

"I was planning on ordering a pizza later. I could call now if you'd like some."

"Would you?"

"Of course." He smiled at his daughter. "I'll get pepperoni with extra cheese." That was Mandy's favorite; he preferred hamburger and onions. But there was no need to buy two.

Max had reached the doorway when she called after him, "You can go on a date when I'm not here, you know. You shouldn't be home alone while I'm gone."

"Where's this coming from?" he asked, forehead creasing.

"Lynn and I were talking. She wondered why you hadn't gotten remarried and I said I didn't know."

"Well, I'd need to meet someone first," he replied. An

image of Terri came to his mind and he brushed it aside. "I'm pretty committed to making this career change. It'll allow us to move if we want."

Their current home was nothing special, just a three-bedroom ranch in a good school district. He'd like something newer, maybe a high-end condo that didn't require as much outdoor work and maintenance. While he didn't mind mowing the lawn and cleaning the gutters, there were a lot of other things he had to do, instead, such as work.

"I like our house," Mandy said, dismissing the idea of moving. She gazed at him pointedly. "Pizza?"

"Ordering," Max told her. He went and tried Lola's phone, leaving her a voice mail asking where she was and when she planned on arriving. Then he ordered a large pepperoni-and-extra-cheese pizza. The store promised a delivery time of thirty minutes or less, so Mandy had a pretty good likelihood of eating before she left.

Max went into the third bedroom, which he used as an office. The living room was the television room, and he'd allowed Mandy to convert the entire family room into Toy Central. While she didn't play with her dolls anymore, they remained a testament to childhood. Now the room also housed her computer, her game system and her books.

The forty-year-old house also had a two-car garage and sat on a standard lot with neighbors fifteen feet on either side. It had been the best he'd been able to afford right out of college, and he often wondered if that had been one of the things to send Lola over the edge.

She'd wanted the glamorous life, but the days of

being around a Final Four college basketball team were long gone. He smiled for a second as he thought of his glory days. He'd been one of the starters on State University's team. They'd only lost two games all season and had become media darlings. Everywhere they went they hadn't had to buy anything. Meals had been free. Drinks. People had wanted his autograph. Guys without girlfriends had plenty to choose from. Excitement surrounded college basketball, especially a Final Four team. Lola had relished the attention and lapped it up. She was queen of the party circuit. The college basketball championships lasted more than a month and had as much media hype as the start of a NASCAR season.

NASCAR season? Where had *that* come from? Terri Whalen again. He had to stop thinking about her.

Max fired up his computer and checked his company e-mail. In January he'd "graduate" the Rising Stars Program. From there, if he played his cards right, he could make all his and Mandy's dreams come true.

His gaze sought the e-mail he wanted, the one from his boss commenting on Max's handling of Terri Whalen's case. He scanned the contents quickly, noting with satisfaction that Brice only had compliments, no criticism. Brice wasn't a man to mince words, so if Max had made a misstep, Brice would have called him on it.

He'd even complimented Max on taking the initiative to handle Terri's case directly, rather than risk her becoming even more frustrated by dealing with random customer-service people. Brice had also approved Max's increasing the settlement offer by the two thousand Terri demanded.

Max read a few more e-mails, a bothersome thought flitting at the back of his brain. When he'd first seen Terri climb out of the car at the race track, he'd had an immediate physical reaction. He'd felt that same flare of interest outside the restroom and then again today when he'd been there as she'd climbed into her truck. He'd hugged her—which was absolutely inappropriate.

Cardinal rule: you don't date clients. Technically Terri wasn't a Rocksolid client, but rather a claimant against the company. And Max didn't want to date her, anyway. She'd just called to his libido, that was all. He'd turned off the sexual side of himself. But for some reason, Terri had brought it flaring to life.

He'd had the urge to kiss her. He dismissed his thoughts as simple longing, caused by being celibate since… Max had lost count of the years. He didn't bother figuring it out, deciding it'd make him depressed.

He focused on the fact that he was a father, not a Lothario. He'd also seen the revolving door that was Lola's love life, and he determined that any woman to whom he introduced Mandy would be special, not just someone he was interested in sleeping with.

Thus, Max had kept his dating life, which really wasn't anything to speak of, away from his daughter. He considered himself once bitten, twice shy. He saw no reason to ever get married again. He'd been there, done that. No use risking another failure. As for Terri, she appeared to be out for thrills and fun. Her truck showed she lived a bit excessively. He'd had enough of Lola and her theatrics. While Terri wasn't exactly an actress, she was involved in the profession as a stunt driver. Max didn't have time for any more drama, and his reaction to Terri proved she could be a complication he didn't need, a diversion from the course he'd plotted and to which he held steadfast.

The doorbell rang and Mandy yelled, "Pizza!"

Max rose to his feet. After Monday he'd never have to see Terri again.

CHAPTER FIVE

TERRI ARRIVED at the Rocksolid Insurance Company office building at three o'clock Monday afternoon. She'd had two early-morning training sessions followed by a four-hour shopping trip with her mother. Somehow she'd managed to squeeze in a five-minute conversation with Max.

All that was left was for her to turn over the title and sign the papers.

Since she'd been out shopping, Terri had worn more than her usual shorts and T-shirt. She'd chosen capris, sandals and a clingy V-neck sweater in peach that made her look tanned even though she really wasn't. She'd achieved that country club air about her today.

The Rocksolid offices were out in the western suburbs in a building constructed within the past five years. The insurance company was the only occupant.

Terri walked through the main doors into a large atrium. She approached a circular desk where a fresh-faced receptionist smiled in greeting. "May I help you?"

"I have an appointment with Max Harper," Terri told her.

"And your name?" the receptionist prompted with an expectant yet friendly smile.

Terri wished she felt half as perky. "Terri Whalen."

"Just one moment." The receptionist picked up her phone and dialed. "Hi, this is Judy in reception. I have a Ms. Terri Whalen to see Mr. Harper."

She gave Terri another smile as she listened for a moment. "I'll tell her."

The receptionist replaced the phone. "Mr. Harper's secretary is on her way down to get you. If you'd take a seat she'll only be a few minutes."

Terri located the seating area and sat on a comfortable chair located near a small waterfall. She gazed toward a bank of elevators on the far wall. She watched as a few people entered, swiped their cards through a scanner and then stepped into the elevator. There were people on the mezzanine above, but she didn't have much time to study them as a thirty-something female who looked about six months pregnant approached. She gave Terri a smile. "Ms. Whalen?"

Terri stood. "That's me."

"Mr. Harper's office is a bit tricky to find, so if you'll please follow me…"

She wasn't kidding. She took Terri to the fifth floor and then started weaving down various short corridors until Terri felt like a mouse in a maze on a hunt for cheese. Finally she stopped and knocked on a partially open door. "Ms. Whalen is here."

"Send her in," Max's deep voice replied, and Terri stepped past his secretary and entered.

She hadn't seen him since Friday, and her body experienced an excited little jolt as he stood and gave her a warm, welcoming smile. "Hi," she said, aware that the secretary had already disappeared.

"Hi. Come on in and have a seat." He'd moved out from behind his desk and came forward to greet her. His handshake was firm, and her body missed his by mere inches as she brushed by him and sat in a chair in front of his desk.

While he reseated himself, she took a moment to glance around the room. It didn't appear as if he spent a lot of time in the interior office. If he did, he was a neat freak, for everything was in its place.

Papers were stacked in the inbox; envelopes ready to be sent in the outbox. He had two bookcases. Two-inch binders lined the three bottom shelves, and framed photos and knickknacks filled the top. Most of the photos were of his daughter Mandy, a few of them of him with her. He had a few autographed NASCAR racing cards—those eight-by-ten driver photos you could find at the track. His cards were several years old—most featured drivers who had retired from racing.

"So you're a NASCAR fan?" she asked.

"I am," Max said, reseating himself and leaning back in his oversize leather chair. He didn't seem in too much of a hurry, and oddly, Terri found herself not wanting to rush, either. Her plan had been to get into Rocksolid Insurance and get out, not to hang out with Max. But she found herself asking, "Are those your favorite drivers?"

"They are, although I must add Billy Budd since he's sponsored by Rocksolid."

"Ah," Terri said with a nod. NASCAR fans were some of the most loyal fans in the world. She knew people who refused to shop at "the other home-improvement store" because they only shopped at the one that sponsored their driver.

"So who does your daughter like?" Terri was curious.

"Anyone who's cute," Max admitted with a laugh that formed dimples in his cheeks. "Mandy is starting to get boy crazy. I didn't think girls got that way at her age, but I've learned I'm wrong. It's starting already."

"What is she? Twelve?"

Max nodded. "Yes. Almost thirteen."

"It'll get worse," Terri said.

"That's what I'm worried about," Max replied.

Terri smiled as she thought of an old memory. "Be happy you got this far. I was boy crazy in kindergarten. My dad wasn't too happy with my antics. Of course, boys had to win against me bike riding or I wouldn't kiss them."

"Boys kissed you in kindergarten?" Max appeared shocked, but in a curious rather than appalled way.

"Just on the cheek," Terri admitted with a laugh, "and it was *me* kissing *them*."

Max relaxed and chuckled. "That's not so bad, then. Pretty innocent."

"Exactly. And it didn't happen often, either, because I dominated anything with two wheels. It was when I started driving four that I had a little trouble."

"Billy told me you raced," Max said.

"For a little while. He was getting into trucks as I was getting out. I don't have that raw talent a driver needs to have to really make it and win. I always had a bit of fear, and you can't have any in this sport. At least, that's what my dad's always saying, and he should know."

"He's Bart Branch's crew chief."

"Yes." Terri had worn her hair loose and the reddish-brown strands swished as she nodded her head.

"I think that'd be a fascinating job, if a little stressful. So was driving in the truck series how you got into stunt driving?"

"It is. I do a lot of odd jobs. I own a fitness studio, I work for one of the driving experiences, and I'm a stunt double. It was my job teaching at the weekend experiences that led me to the stunt work. A producer called up wanting to rent all the cars, and he hired some of the racing experience employees to drive them. We filmed a racing commercial in Nashville."

"So commercials aren't just filmed here in Charlotte?"

She shook her head. "Nope. I go all over. I've been in several movies, all driving a race car. All that footage you see on the big screen has to be filmed. Production companies usually rent the cars and hire the drivers. We're the pros on the track. We know what we're doing because we're drivers in real life. We're just not good enough to make it into NASCAR's Sprint Cup Series on a full-time basis. But there's still plenty of work for us. Those forty-three guys who race every weekend have to concentrate on that, not doing stunt work."

"Wow. That's fascinating," Max said. He shook his head as if a bit embarrassed. "Sorry. I shouldn't be prying into your career. It's only that my ex-wife left me because she wanted to be the next hot thing in Hollywood, and you've had more roles and screen time than she has."

"I'm wearing a helmet," Terri said. "No one ever sees my face. No one even knows it's me." She sympathized with Max. She'd worked on commercials with several people who'd been bitten by the Hollywood bug. But, like race car driving, not everyone had the talent or tenacity needed to succeed.

"I brought my title," she said when the conversation lagged. She reached into her bag to retrieve it—since she'd been shopping, she'd used her oversize bag. She drew out a file folder and removed the document, then passed it to him. "I didn't sign anything yet. I want to look over the settlement papers first."

"That's fine. The title needs the odometer reading, and I had the salvage yard get that for you."

Max checked the front of the title against some paperwork he had on his desk and then turned it over. He wrote the mileage as 23,782. "I'm sorry this happened. Your truck should have had a lot of life left."

"Yeah, I know," Terri said sadly. She read the settlement papers. The documents contained basic contract language saying that once they paid her and she cashed the check, their business was concluded. One of the sections made certain she wouldn't turn around and ask for more money or sue them if she became unhappy down the road. She'd been in a car accident a long time ago when someone had rear-ended her, so she'd seen paperwork like this before. Everything was in order.

Max passed the title back to her and she signed next to where he'd made a small red X.

"The worst thing is that I have no idea what kind of vehicle I want next," she told him. "People think going to get a new car is such fun, but it's really not. I liked what I had. Now I have to go hassle with some guy at the dealership who thinks I'm clueless because I'm female. The last guy I used was great and a friend of my dad's, but he's retired."

"I'm even worse off," he said with a laugh. "I could list everything I know about cars on the end of my thumb."

She suddenly pictured him taking that thumb and sliding it over her bottom lip.

His eyes darkened slightly, making her wonder if he had the power to read minds.

"I have your check here." He opened a file folder, inserted the papers she'd signed, removed the check and handed it over.

Their fingers touched lightly, and then the payoff was in her grasp. She double-checked the amount, which was hers free and clear, as she had no lien on the truck. Then she folded the check, drew her wallet out of her bag, and put the payment inside. She'd go by the bank on her way home and deposit it.

"Thank you," Terri said, realizing that as of this moment, she really had nothing left to say to Max. Rocksolid's payment and her surrender of the title brought their business to an end. Once she stood and walked out the door, he would just be someone with whom she'd once had a business association. They'd talked and been pleasant, but like a plumber coming to fix a broken pipe, they'd remain people whose lives had touched once—to him she'd be just a name of an account he'd handled.

She didn't like that and didn't know why it bothered her so much that she wouldn't be friends with this man. It wasn't like they had anything in common. He wore a suit, worked in an office and had an ex-wife and a kid. She was carefree, worked at multiple jobs and had a schedule dictated only by when her NASCAR clients could fit in workouts around their busy schedules.

"You're welcome," Max replied. "This should conclude everything, but if you have any more questions, don't hesitate to call."

"I'm sure you covered it all," Terri said, inwardly wincing. Had he just given her an opening? He was so hard to read.

"The check was the least we could do," Max said. "Like I indicated before, you've handled this unfortunate situation admirably. I doubt I could have been so collected."

"I'm sure you could have. My brother's son once wrote in permanent marker all over the back rungs of an expensive ladder-back dining-room chair. He put *Dad* on the top, *Mom* underneath, then his name and the words *love* and *family.*"

"Whew," Max said.

Terri smiled at the memory. "Exactly. My nephew ruined the furniture, but my brother said the chair was just stuff. My nephew was trying to say how much he loved his family and wanted to put it out there for everyone to see. I thought my brother would have lost it. But he didn't. He still has the chair and sits on it at every holiday meal."

"It's good you could be practical about your truck," Max said.

Her response was bitter. "Oh, I'm nowhere close. It's hard to say my truck is just stuff, but I'm learning.

Slowly. It's like drivers who crash their favorite race car. It doesn't keep them from racing the next weekend. They have to get over it. So I'm working on doing just that."

"I wish all my company's clients or claimants had your attitude."

Max came around from behind the desk and stood near her. She liked how tall he was, liked that she had to look up to see him. He was broad and built. Was that why she was so attracted? She'd tried this past weekend to meet someone new when she'd been out with Pam, but both nights had been a bust, guy-wise. She really needed to get out there again. Either that or…ask Max out. What did she have to lose?

"If there's nothing else?" Max said.

His secretary had appeared in the doorway.

"No, nothing," Terri said, reaching to shake his hand. His grip was solid in hers and she enjoyed the brief touch.

"Then you have a nice day," Max intoned.

And with that, Terri turned and left both Max and her truck behind.

CHAPTER SIX

THE DAY AFTER turning over her truck title to Max Harper, Terri drove the rental car into Bart Branch's driveway. Bart was the latest driver under her father's tutelage, and unfortunately for her dad, Bart's current season could best be defined as up and down.

Worse had been the fight for morale. Richard Latimer, owner of PDQ, had understood Bart's family issues and given Bart some leeway, but fate had delivered another cruel blow when Richard suffered a massive stroke following the longest race of the year at Charlotte. Six weeks later he'd passed. Not only had Bart lost a boss, a mentor and friend, but he'd also lost some of his mojo.

He'd bounced off the wall and wiped out six cars at Pocono, and after he'd been bumped off course in Daytona, he'd gotten into a fistfight.

Now, heading into the road race at Watkins Glen, the pressure on the drivers on the bubble of making the Chase for the NASCAR Sprint Cup had kicked into overdrive. That meant her father, who was determined to get Bart into the top twelve, had to get his driver into victory lane. Nothing that could give a driver an edge, both in the car and out, was off-limits, especially if it didn't break any NASCAR rules. And that was where Terri came in.

She was here at Bart's house to give him another private three-hour workout in his home gym. In the past Bart had used her studio, but last week he'd installed his own gym and Terri was teaching him how best to use his equipment.

Drivers were certainly a different breed, Terri decided. They loved speed and thrived on adrenaline. Most fans might envy her—she'd had her hands on some of the best-built bodies ever to grace the driver's seat. She'd even helped many wives and girlfriends stay in shape. Keeping them fit and healthy, and mentally sharp, was Terri's expertise.

"Hey," Bart greeted her as he opened the door and Terri stepped inside the two-story-high foyer. Bart had a house on one of the local golf courses, and people could be seen playing the back nine through the windows of the huge great room.

Bart led the way to the basement.

For his warm-up, Terri started Bart on the treadmill. She pressed the grade button, raising the incline to four, and soon had him running at a speed of six miles an hour. He'd do a series of cardio intervals for twenty-five minutes.

"You know I hate this part," he told her, and she laughed at him and set his grade one notch higher.

"Tough," Terri told him, adjusting her headband. Some of her hair had escaped. "You complain every time that you never enjoy this. But the results are worth it."

"If it gets me into the Chase, I'm all for it," Bart said.

"I just don't get a rush from running like I do from driving 180 miles an hour."

"Yeah, but you need this. Already those four hours in the car have you losing eight pounds of water weight per race. You're fit, but you could be in even better cardiovascular shape. Racing's all about endurance and controlling your body."

"And people say we're not serious athletes," Bart remarked.

Terri climbed onto the elliptical machine next to him and started it up. She'd work out alongside him until it was time to hop off and reset his machine. It was better than hovering.

"So what's the status with your truck?" Bart asked as he wiped his forehead with a towel. He tossed it back over the display panel.

"I took their payout. I have to go look for cars this week," Terri told him. "My friend Pam said she'd come with me since Dad's busy."

"She single?" Bart queried.

Terri shot him a disgusted look. "What am I? Your personal trainer or your love connection?"

"Both?" Bart said, giving her a grin that could melt most women's hearts. With curly blond hair, blue eyes and a square jaw, Bart and his twin could make women swoon.

Unfortunately Terri wasn't one of them. Whenever she helped spot Bart with his weights, they'd inevitably touch, and there was no connection. No zing. No wow. No chemistry. She might as well be his sister, which was pretty much the type of relationship they'd developed since her father had become his crew chief.

As for love, Terri wanted someone who'd make her blood heat. Someone who, when he touched her, gave her that zing.

Someone like…

Max's image came to mind and Terri frowned. Yeah, he made her hot and bothered. But he came with baggage she tried to avoid.

She wanted someone single like herself. If she ever did find someone, she wanted to make sure it would last forever, like her parents' marriage. She didn't want to ever endure someone cheating on her. Not that Harry had done that.

She'd broken her engagement to Harry because she'd gotten cold feet. She'd loved Harry, but that *M*-word had meant forever.

Marriage. She couldn't bring herself to take that step with Harry. At that point in her life she was not the forever kind. Her life had been about having fun. Then, men were like shoes. You could try them on for a while and if they didn't fit, you went shopping for a new pair. Even now she refused to give that up until she found the guy who could sweep her off her feet.

Max's image again popped into her head.

"I told you about my friend Pam before, remember?" Terri told Bart now. "She's not into racing. She's a football fanatic. Other than her, all my girlfriends are married or dating someone seriously."

"If she's not into racing, then that won't work," Bart said with mock disappointment. He could speak fine, which meant he wasn't breathing hard. Terri stopped her elliptical and went over to change Bart's treadmill settings.

"You know," Bart cajoled, "I'm not asking for much. Pretty. Loves racing. Likes to have fun. Faithful. Not possessive. Sane—that's always a good quality."

"Ha. You need to concentrate on driving anyway, and bringing home some trophies," Terri said. "There's enough drama in your world without adding women troubles."

"Tell me about it. Each day brings me closer to the damn book that the…" Bart used a not-very-kind word to describe his father's mistress of twenty years.

Terri knew most of the story. Alyssa Ritchie had written an autobiography detailing her life with Hilton Branch, and the advance publicity had shoved the beleaguered Branch family even further into the spotlight. The tell-all book would hit the stores this month, and now Alyssa even had a second book coming out at the same time. News about Alyssa Ritchie seemed to be everywhere. The one who was still unaccounted for was Hilton.

"Relax," Terri urged, deciding to keep Bart on the treadmill for five more minutes to help him unwind. "This is your time to let your body release stress."

Five minutes later Terri reduced his speed to a walk but kept the grade high. After another minute, she lowered the grade to one and reduced the speed again so he could do some lunges.

"How's your mom doing?" she asked. "Lift from the bottom of your foot. That's better."

"My mom's returned to volunteering several days a week at the animal shelter," Bart said. "She's doing it incognito, but it means she's getting stronger and trying to get her life back."

"Well, you're getting stronger, too, and I mean physically. I do think after this session that you're ready for Watkins Glen. You've toned up since I started working with you. You were always muscular, but now those muscles work better."

Bart appeared pleased. "Cool. I'd better be ready. The weather was so hot in Indianapolis that being inside the car that long almost kicked my butt. Being in a uniform can be fatiguing."

"I raced trucks, so I remember," Terri reminded him. "That idea of being cool all over just because my head's got AC isn't everything it's cracked up to be."

"I can't imagine how I survived racing before these sessions. I'm not as worn-out as I was in the beginning."

"Yeah, well, let's make sure your fitness keeps happening. Break's over," Terri replied brusquely, pleased by his compliment.

Done with the cardio portion of the workout, Bart began his weight set. After that, she put him through a combination of yoga and pilates mat work.

"So you'll be there in New York?" Bart asked as the three-hour session came to an end.

"Planning on it. Charles is driving my motor home up for me, so I'll fly there with my dad and the team. I need to do some car shopping."

"Well, good luck," Bart said. "If you need something, let me know."

"You concentrate on racing," she said as he walked her out.

"Yes, ma'am." Bart laughed as he closed the door behind her.

"I WISH I COULD GO," Mandy said as she watched her dad pack his overnight bag.

"It's going to be mostly work," Max replied, hearing his daughter's resigned sigh. He grimaced. While he loved to travel, he didn't like leaving Mandy behind and so had usually wriggled out of any company-required travel. But since this was the Rising Stars Program, and since he was in the PR department, he couldn't get out of the Billy Budd Safe Driving experience Rocksolid was hosting at Watkins Glen.

Since Lola was out of town, too, Mandy would spend part of the weekend at Lynn's house and the rest with Max's mother. That made Max feel a little better. Lola's parenting had been sporadic lately, and Mandy had complained her mother had seemed distant.

Those hadn't been Mandy's exact words, but Max knew his daughter well enough to read between the lines. He wished Lola would stop toying with Mandy. That was one of the reasons Max didn't date much. He didn't want Mandy to get attached to someone who might not be around in a few months. Better for Max to deny himself than have his daughter be devastated by another loss.

He'd fly up to Watkins Glen in a few hours. Rocksolid executives usually flew on commercial airlines, but this time they'd chartered a small six-person plane. Max's weekend schedule involved a track luncheon, making sure the company providing the manpower for the simulator had everything ready, and then a "happy hour" meeting with some of NASCAR's top brass.

Finally he'd watch the race from the suite Rocksolid had rented for the occasion.

He hadn't been to a NASCAR race in years—at least eleven, Max figured. He'd gone to a bunch during his college days, but having a wife and kid had shifted his priorities. Lola hated NASCAR, and she didn't want him spending money on tickets and going without her.

"I'll take you to a race," Max said suddenly as he zipped his bag closed. He had about an hour before he had to take Mandy to Lynn's and depart.

"Really?" Mandy's eyes shone with excitement.

"I'll see if I can get tickets for the NASCAR Sprint Cup Series, which comes back here in October," Max said.

"Thanks, Dad!" Mandy impulsively gave him a big hug and Max held his daughter tight for a moment. It was hard to fathom that in only a few short years she'd be college bound. It seemed like yesterday that she'd been so tiny he could cradle her in his arms.

Grown men weren't supposed to cry, especially in front of their teenage daughters, so when Max released Mandy he turned slightly so she couldn't tell how her hug had affected him. "Get going, you," he told her gruffly. "Make sure you're all packed."

"I am," Mandy said.

"Even your swimsuit?" Max asked.

Mandy's mouth opened into an O. "I forgot that. It's drying in the laundry room. Thanks, Dad."

And with that, they left the room.

MAX, ALAN AND A FEW other Rocksolid suits had arrived Friday night at Watkins Glen and checked into their hotel. Saturday afternoon they'd eaten lunch under a corporate tent before the NASCAR Nationwide Series race had started. Billy Budd had been the guest of honor, and afterward people had dispersed to watch the race. Once the NASCAR Nationwide race ended, Max and Alan had used their credentials and headed to the infield.

Except for the commercial filming, Max hadn't been infield before and he found the entire experience fascinating. He watched as the NASCAR Nationwide Series teams began to load up and leave. Within hours, only the NASCAR Sprint Cup Series haulers and cars remained. They would race Sunday afternoon. He and Alan strolled along, their eyes always open to team movements. During practice, cars would race in and out of the garage area, and you were the one who was supposed to get out of the way.

As they passed Bart Branch's garage space, Max found his gaze scanning the area for Terri. Was she here?

He didn't see her, and he and Alan kept moving, taking in the sights and occasionally stopping to grab those eight-by-ten race cards for their daughters.

They were headed back toward Billy's hauler when Max spotted Terri. She was walking beside Bart and another woman. Max saw Terri at the same time she saw him. Her eyes widened, and as she approached they both stopped.

"Max," she said simply, surprise evident. "What are you doing here?"

"The Billy Budd Safe Driving weekend," Max told her. "Alan, do you remember Terri Whalen? She drove as Billy Budd for the commercials we just made."

"That's why you seem familiar," Alan said, reaching to shake Terri's hand. Bart and the woman at his side had continued on their way. "You did a great job for us. We're very pleased with how the commercials turned out."

"Thank you," Terri said.

Alan suddenly stared past her, toward Billy's hauler. "I see someone I need to speak with."

"I'll meet you in a few minutes," Max said.

"So, here you are," Terri said after Alan walked off.

"Yeah. My first race in forever and my first time in the infield. It's rather…" He paused, at a loss for the perfect word. An energy simply permeated the area.

"Exciting? Different?" Terri prodded.

"All of those. For this month I get to work in PR, and this trip was an unexpected bonus."

She glanced at the driver cards in his hand. "Are those for Mandy?"

"They are," he said.

"You ought to bring her to a race," Terri suggested.

"I'm going to try to get tickets for October. I won't be able to get her credentials, though—she's too young."

"I think the age is eighteen unless you're with someone in the Drivers' and Owners' lot."

"Is that where you are?" Max asked.

"This weekend, yes. I have a motor home that I bring to races within a ten-hour drive. That way I can keep those drivers I train on their workout schedule. I'm actually on my way there now. Bart's got some stretching to do."

"Well, it's been great seeing you again," Max said.

He stood there awkwardly, staring down at the

woman in front of him. He'd thought about her at least once a day since he'd given her her check, which was unlike him.

"You know, this is strange," Terri said, finding her voice. "Since the accident I keep running into you."

"It *is* weird," Max agreed. "Maybe fate's trying to tell us something."

She lifted up her sunglasses and he could see her eyes. "Maybe. So are you here all weekend?"

"I am," Max replied. He shifted his weight. "We're in a suite tomorrow. Want to join us?"

"Do I have to give you my answer now?"

"No. You can call me." Max fumbled for a business card and handed to her.

"I'll think about it," she replied, and with that she moved off.

"So, WHO WAS THAT GUY?" Bart asked as she gave him his workout.

"Oh, no one really. Just one of the Rocksolid PR people. I did some commercial work for them."

Terri moved into a yoga position called "downward dog" and Bart followed suit. He'd race in less than twenty-four hours and yoga would stretch and prep his muscles for the 220-something miles he'd be in the car.

"You seemed into him," Bart said, following her next motion as she moved into a flat-back "plank" position. "And now you're acting like you've got a secret or something."

"You're supposed to be clearing your mind and getting focused on your body, not on my life," she scolded.

She moved back into the "downward dog" position, then walked her feet under her shoulders. She and Bart both hung there, touching their toes. Then they rolled up to a standing position and after a few more positions and deep breaths, the workout was over.

"Man, I feel great," Bart said. He rolled his neck one last time. "I feel like I have all this energy."

"It should keep," Terri told him. "That's the beauty of what we did. You can vary it to either energize or to relax. When you're in the car, remember to do some of the breathing exercises I taught you. It'll help keep you calm and your mind focused."

"I've been trying," he said.

"Like racing, it'll take practice to perfect." She tossed him a bottle of water. "Drink all of that."

"Yes, ma'am," Bart teased. He cracked the top and took a long swallow. "So did you buy a new car yet?"

"No. I looked, and I think I found something I want. I'll buy it next week." Terri grabbed water for herself.

"Getting another truck?" Bart asked.

She shook her head. "I think I'm going to buy some-thing else. Probably an SUV that still tows. Not sure how big I'll go. I'm also trying to get something more fuel-efficient. Help the environment."

"You watching the race from my pit box tomorrow?"

"Max invited me to watch from the Rocksolid suite," she replied.

"You're supporting Billy Budd?"

"No, but Max invited me and that'll free up a space on your pit box. Of course I'm cheering for you. My dad would kill me if I didn't."

"Don't let your loyalties change," Bart warned.

"As if," Terri replied. "Now get out of here and bring home a win this weekend."

TERRI WRESTLED with the idea of meeting Max in the Rocksolid suite. She took his business card out, turned it over several times in her hand. She had no reason to call him. Unless she wanted to see him. She contemplated that for a moment. Max Harper was a good-looking guy. Something about him appealed to her. Maybe it was the way his dark eyes twinkled or maybe she liked his dark hair. But he was divorced. He had a kid.

She continued making her pros-and-cons list in her head. After all, she did like the "suite life," and going with Max would put her high above the action. Sitting in air-conditioning with good food and beverages always made a nice change from her usual seat atop the pit box. She could take a race off from pitbox duties, and Rocksolid still hadn't entirely entered her good graces. Maybe spending time in the suite would ease some of her residual pain over leaving her truck.

Terri leaned back against her sofa. She was being silly. She palmed the card again, and then dialed his cell phone before she lost her nerve. He answered immediately. Oh, how she liked the sound of his voice as he said, "Max Harper."

"It's Terri Whalen."

"Hi, Terri."

She shifted slightly. A man should not be that sexy over the phone, but somehow Max was.

"If the offer is still open, I'd like to join you tomorrow for the race."

"Wonderful. How about I meet you at…" He paused as if checking a ticket. He told her a time and Terri agreed.

"I'll meet you outside on the ground level," Max said.

"I'll see you then." With that, Terri disconnected.

MAX WAS WAITING for Terri when she arrived at the entrance to the suite the next day. They rode the elevator up together. She'd forgotten to ask about the dress code, so she'd dressed in a black knit top and matching pants. She'd worn comfortable pumps. The look wasn't too casual or too dressy. Some suites required high fashion, while others were business casual.

"Terri, you remember Alan Henson, Rocksolid's PR director? You both met briefly yesterday. Terri drove as Billy Budd in our commercials," Max reminded his boss.

"Nice to see you again and I'm glad you could join us," Alan said as he shook Terri's hand. "Max tells me your dad is Bart Branch's crew chief."

"Yes." They talked NASCAR for a few minutes, and then Alan moved away to greet other guests. Over the course of the day Terri learned that most of the people in the suite were top insurance salesmen from around the Northeast. Sprinkled into the mix were wives, girl-friends and a few corporate executives from companies who partnered with Rocksolid.

Max introduced her to everyone, and once the race began, they sat together and watched the proceedings.

"Thanks for joining me," Max said.

"Thank you for inviting me. I'm having fun."

Max grinned. "See, I'm not so bad."

"Maybe not," Terri agreed, allowing herself to flirt with him.

"Perhaps first impressions aren't always the best. You know what they say about judging a book by its cover."

"Yeah, but I'm pretty much 'What you see is what you get,'" Terri replied.

"There's more to you, I'm sure," Max insisted.

Terri conceded. "I guess."

"What are your hopes and aspirations, for example? I mean, do you want to get married? Make more movies?"

She thought for a second. "I'm pretty much set. I'm not looking to get married. I'm a successful business owner and I travel a lot. As for aspirations, well, I think I'm living the dream. You?"

Max shook his head. "Getting there. I'm up for a promotion in January, and if I get that I'll be where I want. It's been a long road for both my daughter and me. She's my world."

Since he'd brought it up… "So no marriage for you, either?"

"Been there, done that. I don't really have much time to date. Work consumes most of my time. I'm determined to stay focused until I succeed. That doesn't mean I don't see my daughter."

"I would never think that. My dad works seven days a week. He rarely takes vacation. That doesn't mean he doesn't make time for my brother or me. He was always there for us, no matter what."

"I'm glad you understand. Not many people do."

"I'm not most people."

"No, you're not and I'm glad of it," Max said, but before he could elaborate, the race entered its final laps and everyone stood to watch the end.

After the checkered flag flew and the race ended, Max escorted Terri back to the security gate. "I guess this is as far as my pass lets me go."

She could get him in, but she knew Alan Henson was waiting. They had a plane to catch. "I had a good time."

"Me, too."

They stood there awkwardly. This was the part of the night Terri hated the most. She wanted to see him again.

"I'm just going to come out and say it," she said. "Ever since I first saw you, I've felt this strange connection between us."

His face reddened slightly and she pressed on.

"Would you like to maybe go get dinner somewhere or something this week? I know you said you don't usually date but…" Terri paused.

"I'd like that." Max beat her to it.

"Well, that's good," she said, her breath coming out in a relieved rush. He'd said yes.

"So, dinner some night?" She stepped toward him, decreasing the space separating them to a few inches. "You do eat, don't you? I believe I saw you with food when we were filming, and today, as well."

He smiled. "I do eat."

"Good. So how about Teddie's?"

Everyone in Charlotte knew where Teddie's was. The place was like Chuck E. Cheese, only for adults. It had video games, billiards, darts and skeeball geared for the twenty-one-and-over crowd.

"How about something calmer?" Max countered. "My mother can watch Mandy, but I'm not up for a lot of noise after work. I know a great Italian place that makes everything on site. Rosie's. Will that work?"

Despite all the delicious food she'd eaten, her stomach grumbled at the suggestion. "I love Italian food. That sounds perfect. Just give me directions and I'll meet you there."

"Why don't I call you with them in the morning and we'll go tomorrow night?"

"I can't do Monday. I'll be driving my motor home and won't get in until late tomorrow. What about Tuesday night, instead?"

Max glanced at his watch, checking the time. "Tuesday's great. I've got to run. I can get your phone number from the file. I'll call you Monday evening once you get back."

"Perfect. Call me after eight and I'll see you Tuesday."

Since Bart had failed to capture the trophy and, instead, placed fifteenth, Terri knew her dad would be disappointed. She went to console him as the team loaded up the hauler.

"You'll get them next weekend," she told her dad, giving him a hug.

Her dad gave her a wan smile. His uniform reeked from the race, but Terri didn't care. Race tracks had their own unique smell, and it was a fragrance only a driver or a fan could love. To her, it was synonymous with her dad.

"Thanks for being here. Bart's at least doing a lot better."

"Five places higher than Indianapolis," Terri reminded him.

"We just need a top ten," her dad said. "You going to be okay driving home?"

"I'll be fine. You know I've done this particular drive before. I'll call you around nine and let you know where I'm at."

"Be sure you do," her dad said, and then with another hug he went to finish tearing down and readying the hauler for transport.

Terri returned to her motor home. She glanced around the garage and toward the stands, which had all but emptied of spectators. She assumed Max had already left the premises.

He'd said he'd call her. A feeling like butterflies erupted in her stomach. She shouldn't feel giddy. Max was a man with a twelve-year-old. He was the type of a guy who was serious about life. He had commitment written all over him. But somehow, he was a pied piper she wanted to follow.

It would only be dinner. How could having a meal hurt?

CHAPTER SEVEN

"WHY ARE YOU SMILING so much?" Mandy asked as she and her dad loaded the dishwasher Monday night.

"I took your advice," Max replied. He gestured, and Mandy added a few plates to the bottom rack. "I'm going on a date tomorrow."

"Huh?" Surprised, Mandy paused in the middle of placing a cup on the top rack. "You met someone?"

Max nodded. "Actually, you've met her, too."

Finished loading, Mandy grabbed the box of dishwasher detergent. "So who is she?"

"She was the lady who drove the Billy Budd car at the filming we attended."

"Really?" Mandy stood there a moment, forgetting she was pouring powdered soap. When she realized she'd overpoured, she jerked the box away, flinging white particles everywhere. "Oops! Sorry, Dad."

"It sweeps up," he told her, thinking of Terri and the story she'd told him about her nephew and the dining-room chair.

"Wow. You aren't going to scold me?" Mandy asked, a bit awed. "Maybe you ought to go on dates more often."

"Ha-ha. Just go get the broom," Max instructed.

He scooped up some of the dry powder with his hands and put it back into the box. Mandy returned with the broom, and soon the floor was clean and the dishwasher running.

"So tomorrow, after school, you'll stay at Grandma's until I come to pick you up," Max said.

Mandy frowned a little. "On Tuesdays Grandma makes meat loaf. It's always dry."

Max chuckled. "Your grandma can cook better than I can, and you don't have to eat everything she piles on your plate. She used to cook for all us boys when we were growing up. We ate triple helpings of everything. Even meat loaf. Your grandfather likes his meat loaf to have tons of breadcrumbs in it. Just put some ketchup on it—that's what I do."

"Grandma also likes to try to fatten me up. She keeps telling me I'm too skinny and I need meat on my bones," Mandy said. Max gazed at his daughter. She was in that preteen state where her body was beginning to change. She certainly wasn't too skinny.

"She means well," Max said, defending his mother. "But don't you worry, I'll call her and ask her not to make you clean your plate."

"Thanks." Mandy's relief was obvious. "I hate making her feel bad when I don't like something."

"I know," Max said, reaching out to ruffle his daughter's hair. "Grandma can be a bit overbearing at times. Growing up, your uncles and I were a handful. She learned to outgun us."

"Dad, not the hair." Mandy tried to straighten it.

"Last time you got together, Uncle Brent ended up with a black eye."

"Yep, and Aunt Ruth wasn't too happy about that, either," Max said.

Every Thanksgiving, no matter what the weather, everyone played football. In the summer, he and his brothers played basketball out on the driveway. The games could get pretty energetic—no one wanted to admit they weren't as agile as they'd been twenty years ago.

"So where you going on your date? And by the way, what's her name?" Mandy asked.

"Her name is Terri and we're going to Rosie's."

Mandy nodded. "That's a good place. Will you bring me back some fettuccine? That way I can skip the meat loaf and not be hungry."

"I can bring you something if you promise to eat some meat loaf, anyway," Max said. "Now go get your room cleaned. You also need to scoop out the cat litter."

Mandy made a face that showed him exactly what she thought about her chores.

"Go," Max commanded, suppressing a smile. "If not, you can't watch TV and I'll make you go to bed early. You know I mean it."

"Fine," Mandy said, and left for her room.

Max finished straightening up the kitchen. He still needed to phone Terri and give her directions. He also needed to call his mother and ask her if she and his dad could keep Mandy a bit longer than they usually did at night during the summer.

His mother had been a real blessing in Max's being able to raise Mandy. His parents lived nearby, and Max dropped his daughter off every day. Jean Harper made sure Mandy had breakfast, and then took Mandy to school when she wasn't on vacation.

Max wasn't certain how he felt about his daughter being in middle school. All he knew was the years had slipped by so fast. Now she was into things like talking on her cell phone, posting to friends online and wearing lip gloss. The latter two, thankfully not too much. He had a feeling the upcoming years were going to be a real challenge. Soon she'd be off to college. And then out on her own.

He headed into the television room, where he picked up the phone and dialed Terri's number.

"TERRI WHALEN," Terri said, answering her cell phone despite the fact that she was bent over touching her toes when it rang.

"Hey. It's Max Harper."

Terri straightened quickly, something she always chided her clients for doing. When he'd called earlier, she'd still been in the middle of traffic and so hadn't answered the phone. His voice mail said he'd call back, and now he had. She attempted to sound casual. "Hi."

"I wanted to take a minute before Mandy and I watch TV," he said, "and give you directions to Rosie's. I'm looking forward to seeing you tomorrow night."

Which meant the date was still on. Terri experienced a sense of relief. She'd been on pins and needles, wondering if he'd back out.

She knew she was simply being paranoid, but she hadn't been this nervous since she was thirteen and had kissed a boy—on the lips—for the first time in a truth-or-dare game.

"Directions would be great," Terri said, trying to catch her breath. The drive from New York always stiffened her up and she'd been doing yoga to loosen her muscles.

However, that wasn't the only reason her body was all worked up. To slow her racing heart, she'd need to do more positions once she got off the phone. Just hearing his voice had an effect on her.

"Do you have a pen and paper?" Max asked.

A bit discombobulated, Terri grabbed both. "Yup," she said as she clutched them in her fingers.

"Great. Where are you coming from?"

She told him, and soon she'd jotted down directions to Rosie's. "I'll meet you there at five-thirty. Will that work?" she asked.

"Yes. I also promised I'd bring Mandy back some fettuccine. My mom cooks meat loaf every Tuesday and Mandy's not a fan."

"My mom always changed the menu around. We never knew what she'd serve, only that my brother and I had a non-negotiable dinnertime. If my dad wasn't out of town, we gathered around the dinner table like the Waltons."

"That's not a bad thing. I try to have family dinnertime with Mandy, but between work and her guitar lessons and her dance class, we're everywhere. Dinner often comes in a bag through the car window."

"Yes, but you can talk in the car," Terri said. "You have a captive audience."

"I bet you never ate in that truck of yours," Max said.

"No," Terri admitted. He'd pegged her correctly.

"Food goes everywhere. I admit, I was a bit overprotective of my truck, for all that got me."

"I'll buy you a nice dinner to make up for your car-shopping woes," Max teased. "Right now I need to go and make sure Mandy's doing her chores. If she gets on the Internet, she can lose track of time. We're working on that. I'll see you at Rosie's. I'm looking forward to it."

"Me, too," Terri said, and suddenly the phone in her hand went dead, the call disconnected.

The entire conversation hadn't lasted more than five minutes, but in that short time she'd learned Max valued family and monitored his daughter's activities.

Terri set the phone down and gazed at herself in the floor-to-ceiling mirrors. Was that the reason for her attraction to Max? Because he had family values similar to hers?

Terri really didn't know the answer to her question, so she concentrated on pushing her body to the limit, preparing it to indulge in good food and hopefully good company the next day.

MOST RESTAURANTS didn't get crowded the minute they opened, but the moment she entered Rosie's, Terri realized she'd totally misjudged the place. She'd expected something along the lines of a quiet little family establishment. Already there was a one-hour wait, the first patrons having been seated at five. Rosie's was a Charlotte hot spot.

Max was already in the bar, and she easily located him, as he towered over many of the others. She wove her way in his direction and swallowed when she reached him.

The cut of his suit emphasized his muscular body, and she was a woman who knew men's physiques. "Hi," she said, suddenly nervous.

Max turned and gave her a high-wattage smile that melted Terri's insides. "Hey. Glad you found the place okay. What would you like to drink?"

"Chardonnay is fine," Terri replied, and soon he handed her a wineglass. In his hand he held a short tumbler of a dark liquid. Some sort of whiskey blended with cola, Terri thought. "So I thought we were going someplace quiet?"

"We are. Our table's ready. It's this way," Max said, leading her into the actual restaurant portion. Even here the atmosphere hummed as diners conversed, but the sound was more muted. Max led her to a corner booth. Terri noted that every table was occupied.

"This must be a popular place," she said.

He arched an eyebrow. "You've never been here? Some of the best Italian food in the area. My aunt and uncle own this place."

"No wonder Mandy wants carry-out."

Max grinned. "Yep. Mom's sister got the cooking talent. My mom's got skills, and she's a much better cook than I'll ever be, but she can't cook as well as my aunt Terese."

"So you're Italian?" Terri asked. Maybe that explained his tall, dark and handsome good looks.

He grinned. "No, I'm not. Terese's husband is, and Rosie's is named for his mother. I'm not really sure what the Harper clan is. When it comes to genealogy and ancestry, we can't trace ourselves back to the *May-*

flower or anything. No one's ever had any interest in pursuing our family tree. In this day and age, it doesn't seem to matter. What about you?"

"A bit Irish. Maybe some English. I never thought much about ancestry, either," she admitted.

She took a sip of wine as a waiter dressed in a dinner jacket approached. "I guess we should take a minute to look at the menu."

"I already know what I want, but please take all the time you need to decide. If you have any questions, ask. I've had most everything." He gestured with his glass, urging her to pick up her menu.

"Figures you'd know everything," Terri said.

"It's all delicious. Trust me."

Terri opened the menu, which had four pages. She had no clue what to eat. Everything sounded wonderful.

"Okay, I'm ready to order," she said finally.

"You're sure?" Max asked, his tone light. She'd taken five minutes to read everything, not wanting to rush her decision. He'd waited patiently, without interrupting her, the whole time.

"This was hard. Too many delicious options," Terri protested as the waiter returned, carrying a basket of bread.

Eating one slice would be pure indulgence on her part. Bread tasted wonderful, but it was high in bad carbohydrates. Tonight, however, she decided she didn't care. Max was the most invigorating man she'd met in a while. She might as well let go and fully enjoy herself.

The waiter took their order and left.

"So does your family know you're on a date with me?" Terri asked.

Max nodded, the recessed lights dancing off his dark hair. "Mandy does. And as for my aunt and uncle, they've given you the once-over already, but they pride themselves on their discretion. I'll get the third degree next weekend when everyone's at my brother's birthday party."

"So family events are a big deal?" Terri asked, reaching for the bread. It was still warm.

"The biggest. We all live within thirty miles of each other. We're constantly doing something. There's always someone's birthday or wedding anniversary or something like that."

The idea of so many family gatherings boggled Terri's mind. "Wow. I can't remember the last time my family all got together, aside from major holidays. We don't do too many get-togethers. I only see some of them on Thanksgiving, Christmas and Easter. My cousins? I don't really even know them. My dad's off racing for most of the year. We do celebrate my parents' birthdays and anniversaries, but I haven't been to an event for my brother in years. My niece and nephews, yes. But not as often as I'd like. I'm usually on the road with my dad."

Terri had always wondered if the Whalen family was a bit dysfunctional in that they didn't have big family gatherings. Then again, it was hard when you were on the road ten months of the year.

"My dad and I are close, and I love my mom, and my brother and his family," she said. "That's really all that matters."

"Exactly." Max withdrew a slice of bread and buttered it.

Terri's mouth watered, and not because she had yet to sample the piece she still held in her hand. Max could pay the check and take her home right now, so long as there was a lot of kissing involved. She shook her head slightly, trying to clear her mind of such dangerous thoughts. She liked Max, and the last thing she wanted was a one-night stand, no matter how much electricity seemed to zing between them.

Then again, the connection between them was more than that. It went beyond the sexual, although admittedly her physical desire for this man was intense.

Terri might like to live life footloose and fancy-free, but with Max she feared making any misstep, including rushing anything.

"Are you okay?" Max asked, noticing her silence.

"I'm savoring," Terri lied, biting into the bread. As if sensing she needed respite, the waiter approached with their salads. She concentrated on eating for the next several minutes, occasionally asking Max questions to start him talking about himself.

Over the course of the evening, he told her about his company's Rising Stars Program, his daughter's guitar playing and more about his immediate family. Like her brother, each of Max's brothers also owned his own business. One owned a construction company and the other a bakery.

"He supplies all the bread and desserts for Rosie's," Max told her. He gestured to her chicken piccata. She'd almost cleaned her plate. "Make sure you save some room for cake. It's one of his specialties."

"I will," Terri promised. She was already stuffed and

her belly seemed to press against the waistband of her pants. If the average serving was approximately the size of a man's fist, she'd eaten at least three when counting bread, salad and the chicken entrée.

Normally she didn't eat this much. At home she might eat an apple and a salad for dinner and couple that with a handful of almonds. Her biggest meal was usually breakfast, where she indulged a bit more, adding oatmeal or poaching an egg.

"So you have a family party this weekend?" She returned the conversation to that topic.

"No, the following Friday night. My oldest brother is turning forty," Max said. "Marvin's the first one to reach the big four-o."

"I'm not even thirty yet," Terri said with a small shudder.

"And I've got seven years left to that milestone," Max said. "You could come to the party if you'd like."

She tilted her head and gave him a sympathetic smile. "Thanks for the offer, but I'm going to be at Bristol for the race." The Michigan race was next, but it was too far for Terri to drive, so Bristol would be her next stop.

"When will you leave?"

"Early Saturday morning. It's only four hours."

"So you could attend if you wanted," Max said.

Terri didn't know what to say. Meeting his family seemed too sudden and too much of a commitment. When she'd become engaged to Harry, she'd only met his family once. She and Harry had always been on the road.

"So you go to all the races?" Max asked, changing the subject.

Terri nodded. "Most of them. My motor home doubles as a fitness studio. Some tracks, like the one in Texas, have facilities the drivers can use if they want. My place is much more private, and many of my clients feel more comfortable having me there."

He leaned forward. He'd long ago finished his pasta. He'd only had the one alcoholic drink, moving to straight cola for his subsequent beverages. "It has to be a whole different world. Sort of like being part of a celebrity entourage. I found all the infield stuff fascinating."

She fingered the stem of her second glass of wine, one she'd been nursing for about an hour. "It can seem crazy. Really, though, all the guys are much more grounded than those Hollywood types, who always seem to be in and out of rehab. The drivers are just doing what they love, which is driving really fast. Watkins Glen is a road course, so that's a bit different than being on an oval like Bristol. Bristol's a short track and it's always an exciting race."

"I've never driven over ninety miles an hour, and that was back in college in a friend's car," Max said. "I guess I've never been bitten by the speed bug. I'm the ultimate insurance-statistics guy."

"Well, these guys are professionals. You should try one of the driving schools. I teach at one occasionally. I could check and see when the next one's in Charlotte."

"That might be an idea," he said.

She took a sip of wine. "My personal opinion is that everyone needs to be out on the track at least once. It's an absolute rush."

"So have you done bungee-jumping?" Max asked.

Terri shook her head. "No. Why? Have you?"

"No. I'm just seeing if there's anything you haven't done." Max smiled. "You seem to like adventure."

"I do, but I also like my feet, or at least four tires, on the ground," Terri told him, appreciating his attempt at humor.

The waiter appeared and they ordered a slice of chocolate cake for her and a slice of a vanilla-custard cake for him.

"Do you want coffee?" Max asked, turning over his cup as the busboy came by with a coffeepot containing decaf.

"I don't drink coffee or tea," Terri admitted. "I've attempted a sip, but I can't stand either."

"Probably healthier in the long run, but I couldn't get through the morning without a strong cup of java. I don't need the caffeine now." He added a packet of sugar to his cup, then cream. He saw her gaze. "I'm secure enough in my manhood not to need to drink it black. It's a tad bitter."

"Which is why I don't like it." She spotted the waiter coming their way, two plates of cake in his hand. "Dessert's here."

The waiter set the chocolate cake in front of Terri.

"This looks fantastic," Terri said, lifting a forkful to her lips as Max took a moment to check on Mandy's carry-out order. The chocolate flavor rolled over her tongue and she sighed.

"Good?" he asked.

"Mmm. Delicious. Worth the extra mile I'll need to run. Tell me, is your brother married?"

Max laughed. "Yes, he is. You're stuck with dating me."

"But you don't cook," Terri said, closing her eyes for a second as she savored the velvety taste.

"No, but I have connections and can get you any pastry your heart desires by lifting my finger and making a phone call."

"Sold. That's good enough," Terri said. She opened her eyes and found him watching her. "What?"

"Just enjoying the view," Max said. She blushed. He seemed to really appreciate her. When they talked, he truly listened and was interested in what she had to say, unlike some guys she'd met. She'd enjoyed herself, and decided that despite her former aversion to divorced men, she wanted to see him again, even if it meant taking the initiative herself.

She finished her dessert. "So, this has been an okay date? Even though you picked the place, if I asked you out again, you'd say yes?"

"I think so," Max said. "There's always my brother's birthday party."

An idea formed. Terri had never done anything like this before, but the more the idea gelled, the more she liked it. "So aside from your brother's party, what are you doing the rest of that weekend?"

"Whatever it is, I have Mandy," he said.

"Then how about coming to Bristol with me?" she suggested.

His tone contained disbelief. "As in go to Tennessee?"

She nodded, her hair swishing around her chin. "Yes. You, me and Mandy. It's an easy drive and it's the ultimate short track. We can leave Saturday morning. I have the motor home."

"The one with the studio."

"Yes, but it also sleeps five. I can get Mandy into the garage area. As for my work, I have about four hours each day when I have training. The rest of the time I can be your and Mandy's tour guide. What do you say?"

"I'll have to ask Mandy and see what she thinks," Max replied.

"Do. The race is Saturday night under the lights. We can work out the details later."

The waiter came by with the carry-out order and the bill. "Thank you," Max told the man. He nodded at Terri. "I'll ask her and call you."

"I need to get passes for you, so the sooner I know the better," Terri said.

"That's fine. I know I'd really like to go. Mandy's never been to a race."

"I think she'll love it," Terri said.

"Thank you for including her," Max said.

Terri frowned. "Why wouldn't I?"

Max shook his head, letting his motion be her answer. Maybe the women he'd dated didn't want Mandy hanging around?

"You're special," he said, "do you know that?"

"Oh, don't you go getting all serious on me," Terri said, flattered yet at the same time frightened. "I don't handle *serious* very well. I'm all about keeping things light and fun. Racing fits both. You strike me as a guy who could use a little fun in his life."

The waiter appeared and Max handed him his credit card. "So is that all this is?" he asked, gesturing with the bill holder. "Some fun for Max?"

"No," Terri said. She scowled for a second as she tried to understand the shift in the mood. "I don't do charity cases, if that's what you're insinuating."

Max shook his head. "No, that's not what I'm saying. But I need you to clarify your intentions. I'll admit that I like you. I like being with you. But at my age and my circumstances, I have to be up-front and lay my cards on the table. I have a daughter to worry about. Unlike my ex-wife, I've tried not to have a series of relationships. I don't want Mandy to get attached to a woman in my life only to have the woman disappear when the fun's gone. I've never introduced her to any of the women I've dated."

Terri sat back against her chair. "Whoa. I didn't see that coming."

He gave her a wistful smile. "Sorry to ruin things. Now you know why I don't date much. I usually get about this far and blow it."

She mulled over his words for a moment, putting herself in his shoes. Max had depth, and it was as refreshing as it was petrifying. However, she didn't want to walk away from him yet.

"No, you didn't ruin anything," Terri said finally. "I appreciate candor. I like your being up-front. It's a nice change from players who think life's just a big game. I may like to be carefree, but I'm not frivolous. I don't do casual."

"I'm not a party animal. I had to leave that life behind when Mandy came along," Max said.

"I'm still able to pick up and go," she said. "I guess that makes us opposites." She studied him. She liked the way his eyebrows arched, and the way the lights reflected off his black hair. He was extremely handsome. "Do you think that's why we're attracted to each other? Because we're so different?"

"Perhaps," Max conceded. "I admit to not having a clue. But I don't want to stop seeing you. I sense something."

Terri sighed. "I do, too. But I'm not here because of physical attraction."

"Ah, good to know you want me for my mind." He faked a short laugh.

"Not that I don't want other things," Terri said quickly, deciding to match his honesty with some of her own. "Your body does things to mine. I get around you and short-circuit."

"Likewise," Max said.

"So…Bristol?" Terri asked.

"I can tell you yes or no tomorrow," Max said.

After signing the bill and putting his credit card back in his wallet, he put his hand on the carry-out box. Terri gestured at it. "As much as I'm sure we'd both like to linger," she said, "we should probably get going. You have to work tomorrow and Mandy needs to eat."

"True, and Mandy probably would prefer her food to be somewhat hot," Max said with a small smile. He didn't move yet and, instead, said, "If nothing else and Bristol doesn't work out, let's do dinner again when I don't have to rush off. I would like to get to know you better."

"I'd enjoy that," Terri replied. She wanted to find out where things with Max would lead. He was so wrong for her, but somehow, everything felt so right.

They left the restaurant, and he walked her to her rental car. "At least it's an SUV," he said.

"I have to buy something tomorrow. Something about my rental days running out."

"Rocksolid only gives you so long to purchase a new vehicle once they've given you a settlement check. Most insurance companies are like that," Max said.

"So I've learned." Terri unlocked the car using the wireless remote. "So how long would you give me?"

"How long do you want?" Max said. They were no longer talking about the rental-car period, but rather, relationship length.

Such a loaded question for a first date. But oddly the answer that came to Terri's mind was *Forever.*

Which was silly, for she'd never been a forever type of girl. The last time she'd faced any type of permanent commitment, she'd turned around, given Harry back his engagement ring and run away as fast as she could.

"Just tell me you'll give me a quick kiss good-night," she said instead, allowing him the opening for something they both wanted.

He leaned toward her, entering her space. He towered over her and then, ever so gently, raised her chin with his fingers and brought his lips down to hers.

He tasted better than chocolate cake was Terri's last cognizant thought as his mouth explored hers. She reveled in the feel of him, the gentleness of his lips, the teasing of his tongue. Then he was pulling back, the August air cooler than the heat burning between them.

"I'll talk to you tomorrow," he said, stepping aside so Terri could climb into her car.

"Tomorrow," she echoed, and she wobbled slightly on the heels she'd worn, a concession to his height. She managed to get inside, crank the engine and put the car in Reverse. It was still early, and nightfall nowhere close.

She saw him clearly as he stood there, waiting and making sure she'd backed up safely. Then he waved and walked to his car, carry-out bag in hand. As Terri drove away, both giddiness and doubt crept in. The kiss had knocked her socks off. She wasn't an angel and she'd been around the track a few times. She'd thought herself in love before, but hadn't been ready to give up her freedom.

So what had made her ask Max to Bristol? Max was Mr. Serious. She was Ms. Footloose-and-Fancy-Free. The race track was her playground. She had the sudden insight that she was already in way over her head.

CHAPTER EIGHT

MAX THOUGHT about Terri and their date the entire way to his parents' house. Except for when his college basketball team had played in the Final Four championship game, he'd never felt quite so alive as he had tonight. He'd loved talking with her and joking with her.

He appreciated her fun-loving spirit. He liked the way her hair danced around her chin and her greenish-hazel eyes twinkled in the candlelight.

She was right—this had to be a case of opposites attracting. Try as he might to do otherwise, he wanted to see her again. He parked the sedan and entered the kitchen of his childhood home, ready to face the inquisitors.

"Here you go," Max said to Mandy, holding the white paper bag as he entered.

"You're home early," his mother said. Max gave his mom a quick kiss on the cheek before he passed the food to his daughter.

"I told Mandy I'd bring her something," Max explained.

"Which is probably why she didn't eat much," Jean chided. She glared at him for a second. "I'll forgive you this time, but next time you must let me know when you're feeding her."

"I will, promise," Max said. His father loved meat-oaf sandwiches, so it wasn't as if any of tonight's leftovers would go to waste.

"So how did your date go?" Mandy had the container open and was forking food into her mouth.

"Slow down," Max said as Mandy made a slurping sound with the white-sauce-covered noodles.

"Sorry." A bit of the food was stuck to her chin.

He winced and reminded himself to work more on her manners. Mandy reminded Max of the way his brother Brent used to eat at that age. Mandy already had enough tomboy in her.

Like Terri. However, while Terri might fit into a guy's world with her truck and racing, she didn't eat like she was starving. Mandy *could* be more ladylike.

"So," Mandy prodded him, continuing to eat, but in a more mannerly fashion.

"We had a great time," Max replied.

"Good," his mother said, touching him on the shoulder. "You deserve to have a nice evening. What's she like?"

"She's a stuntwoman," Mandy said.

Jean's left eyebrow rose, her nonverbal movement saying, *Please not another one in show business.*

Max worked to reassure his mother. "She's also a personal trainer. She's a one-woman business. Her father's a crew chief in NASCAR. That's how she got into driving. She raced in the truck series for a while."

"Oh." Jean appeared a little less worried, but not by much. Max grimaced. He hadn't had a good track record in choosing the right women to date. Lola was proof enough.

"It was only a first date," he said defensively.

"So will you go out with her again?" Mandy had devoured half the fettuccine and she looked expectantly at her father.

Max still had a warm feeling from the date, so he nodded. "I hope so. She asked us if we'd like to attend a race."

Mandy's eyes widened. "Really? Both of us? Not just you?"

He was suddenly grateful that Terri hadn't asked only him. Most women he'd dated had seen Mandy as a third wheel, which is why one date was usually his limit. "Yes. At Bristol. You and me."

"In Tennessee?" his mother asked, making a rhyme.

Max kept his gaze on Mandy so he could gauge his daughter's reaction. She seemed pretty excited. "Yes. Bristol, Tennessee. Terri has a motor home. We'll go up Saturday morning. That way we can attend Marvin's birthday party. She'll get us passes so we can go everywhere. Even Mandy can go infield."

"It sounds exciting," his mother said. "And you could skip the birthday party."

"Could we?" Mandy asked. "I'd rather go to the track."

"Your brother won't mind," Max's mom said. "You know he loves NASCAR. He'd probably wish he was you. Bring him back an autograph and he'll be thrilled."

"I'll have to ask Terri. I do have some vacation time if we want to drive over Friday, instead of waiting until Saturday."

"Lynn's always saying that Bristol's the best short-track racing," Mandy said. "She'll be steamed that I'm going and not her. Do you think I can meet some more of the drivers?"

"Terri knows a lot of them, like Bart and Will Branch. She's Bart's personal trainer."

Mandy scrunched up her face. "What's that?"

"A fitness instructor. Sort of like your gym teacher, but she works one-on-one," he said.

"Oh. Well, Bart Branch is cool. I like him better than Will. Although you really can't tell them apart since they're identical. Lynn likes Will better. We decided we can each have a twin."

"Since when did you start following NASCAR?" Jean asked Mandy.

"Oh, Dad's always loved it and so does Lynn. After I met Billy Budd, I figured I'd check NASCAR out a bit more," Mandy said. "You know, keep up with everyone and everything."

Max shook his head. His little girl sounded so rational and mature. But beneath her words, Max knew the boy-crazy years had started.

WEDNESDAY MORNING, the following week, Max's phone beeped. "You have a call on line one," his secretary relayed.

Without thinking and expecting Terri, Max reached for it. While they'd spoken on the phone, he hadn't seen her since that night at Rosie's as their schedules hadn't meshed. "Max Harper."

"Max."

Lola. Max inwardly cringed at the sound of his exwife's voice. "Is something wrong?"

"Of course not. Can't your ex call you up when she needs to talk?" Her voice was light and airy, so different from Terri's fun, yet grounded-in-reality tone.

"I'm working," Max said patiently. He had a stack of things to do, especially if he planned on taking Friday off.

"You're always working," Lola replied. "We could have talked last night, but Mandy said you were out."

"I was," Max responded vaguely. He'd been at a work-related dinner meeting.

"Max," Lola said, her tone petulant, "we need to talk. When can we meet?"

"I'm really busy," he stated.

"You're always busy," Lola replied, but he could hear the steel in her voice. She was getting frustrated with his short answers.

Lola's behavior was highly predictable: she'd hem and haw, then she'd blow up, next she'd threaten him, and finally she'd make herself—and him—miserable with her theatrics.

She'd also take her rage at him out on Mandy, only she'd do it in subtle, underhanded ways like belittling Max in various innocent-sounding statements designed to undermine his worth as a father. The pattern had been going on for ten years, and nothing he'd done, including a legal warning, had stopped it.

He'd certainly tried to stop Lola from behaving the way she did. However, he'd failed to do so during their marriage, and there was no reason his ex-wife would change now. Old habits died hard.

"I thought we could meet somewhere," she continued. "Do dinner. Talk. My mother can watch Mandy tonight, so we can have some alone time. Mandy's getting older. We really need to talk about her becoming a teenager."

Max really had nothing to say to Lola. She'd flit into Charlotte, stay awhile and disrupt everything. Then her agent would call and she'd be gone again.

Already she'd brought a black cloud to his day. "This week is a total bust," he told her. "I can't get out of my work commitments. What about next week?"

"Tonight would be perfect," Lola said. "I've arranged everything."

"Well, it's not perfect," Max replied, trying to remain patient. "You should have consulted me before you made any plans."

"I'm consulting you now. I thought it wouldn't be such a big issue."

Max sighed. Lola never thought of anyone but herself. If she wanted something, she demanded it occur on her timetable. Unfortunately life didn't work that way.

"Lola, it's not that I don't appreciate your effort, but tonight is not an option." And certainly, nor were any of the rest of the days of the week.

"Mandy tells me you're going out of town this weekend," Lola said suddenly.

Ah, Max thought. This was probably what the call was really about.

"Yes. We're going with a friend of mine to watch the NASCAR races at Bristol."

"I don't think that's a good idea." Lola's tone turned icy.

Max suppressed a sigh of frustration. Lola didn't like anything she hadn't thought of herself.

"It will be fine," Max said, knowing that Lola couldn't legally stop him from taking the trip. "Look. I have to get back to work. I'll talk to you later."

With that, he set the receiver down and programmed his phone to direct any calls to voice mail. He did have a meeting to attend. He rose, grabbed his stuff and tried to put his ex-wife out of his head.

LOLA SOMERS fumed as she set down the phone. She angrily tapped her fingers against the arm of the chair. She'd settled down with a cup of green tea, thinking she'd have a nice conversation with Max.

She wasn't too pleased with his reaction. She was less pleased with what Mandy had told her last night when she'd called—that she and her dad were going to watch a NASCAR race with one of Max's friends.

The last thing Lola wanted was for Mandy to get hooked on that sport. NASCAR races weren't Lola's preferred entertainment. Sitting courtside at a basketball game—now that was classy. All the stars did that.

No one saw you in a race track suite.

But what really bothered her was that Mandy had told her the person they were traveling with was female. That stunt driver Mandy said she'd met. The one with more acting credits than she, Lola, had—even if no one ever saw the woman's face. Lola thought for a moment, remembering the details. Terri. That was her name.

Lola seethed more, her fingertips increasing their tempo as her agitation grew. She stood and studied herself in the floor-length bedroom mirror, noting her long raven-black hair and her almost black eyes. She leaned forward and lifted the edge of one perfectly plucked eyebrow. Already, at age thirty, the wrinkles were starting to show.

Lola knew she couldn't keep this up forever, even if she found someone else to foot the plastic-surgery bill as she had last time. Maybe she wasn't destined to be Hollywood's hottest star. If that was the case…

She snapped her fingers. Max could not be moving on. He'd never dated anyone seriously for the past ten years. She'd always assumed it was because he hadn't gotten over her. She had been the one to leave him, after all. She wanted to pursue her acting career, and she'd been trapped in Charlotte.

She loved her daughter, but having a child in Hollywood was like having a ball and chain. So she'd let Max raise her.

Now that Mandy was older, she needed a woman's touch. Mandy didn't care about the latest fashion or social graces. That was her ex's poor influence. He'd refused to give Mandy the Christmas presents she'd sent, saying fancy underwear for little girls was not appropriate.

Max. Lola took a second to reflect on her ex-husband. He'd done the right thing by marrying her when she'd gotten pregnant, but she'd wanted to soar, not play house. She'd never wanted to trap him, and the pregnancy had been accidental. Despite the dishes she'd lobbed at his head during their tenure, she'd been certain she'd broken his heart when she left. And she had no doubt she could win him back if she tried.

Unlike the falseness of Hollywood, Max offered a sort of gentle respect. He'd always been so tender. She admitted to missing that. He must *not* have gotten over her or he'd have married again. He'd had ten years to find someone.

Lola ran her hands over her hips, smoothing the tunic-length shirt she wore over leggings. If Hollywood didn't pan out, she certainly didn't want to live alone for the rest of her days.

And if they got back together, Mandy would have her family back. Max had to understand what was truly at stake—their daughter's ultimate happiness.

Lola was determined that she and Max would talk. As for Terri, Lola would handle the situation. She had no problem with that at all.

CHAPTER NINE

BRISTOL, TENNESSEE, was home to one of those race tracks that sold out year after year.

"It's a lot smaller than the track near home," Mandy observed as Terri drove up to a security gate. Mandy sat on the couch and stared out the window, as she'd done for the latter part of the journey, which had started at seven Friday morning when Terri had rolled her big motor home down Max's street.

Terri had found the drive through suburbia rather interesting, as she'd grown up on acreage up near Mooresville.

When she'd arrived, Max and Mandy had been ready to go. They'd climbed aboard and for the first thirty minutes of the trip, Mandy had been excited and bouncy. She'd explored every inch of the motor home, discovering that the front contained the living and kitchen areas.

The couch converted to a queen-size bed once the slide-outs were extended. The middle section of the home also had a slide-out and contained a compact workout studio, and the back section comprised the bedroom and bathroom.

After Mandy had declared Terri's motor home the

best way to travel, she'd settled down and watched a movie on the plasma screen, the novelty of the drive wearing off quickly.

Unlike smaller RV units, Terri's motor home was the size of a tour bus and thus didn't have a passenger seat up front next to the driver. Max had had to sit behind Terri while she drove. It had made conversation difficult, and eventually she'd suggested he read if he wanted. However, now that they'd arrived onto race track grounds, he'd moved to stand on the steps.

"So we're about there?" Max asked.

"Yep," Terri replied, stopping to show her hard-card credentials to a security guard. "We'll be staying in that fenced-in lot over there."

Max followed her gaze. "Those look like haulers."

"They are. The NASCAR Sprint Cup Series haulers get to be infield, but the NASCAR Nationwide Series haulers are outside. It's interesting, but somehow it all works out."

Terri followed the track workers, who used batons and directed various vehicles this way and that. The haulers had arrived Thursday night in a big parade down State Street. The motor homes came in today—Friday—and tonight. Terri, Max and Mandy had seats in the stands for the NASCAR Nationwide race. She owed that good fortune to Anita Wolcott, Bart's PR rep.

As for Bart, Terri had scheduled him a two-hour workout both today and tomorrow during some of his free time. By a twist of fate, his motor home was in line two places behind her, so they'd be parked pretty close together.

Not that Bart Branch would have much free time. Terri had a complete copy of Bart's schedule, and Anita had him coming and going. Not only did he have his required racing practices and qualifying, but he also had three different sponsor events to attend.

Admittedly, Bart's sponsors were still a little bit nervous, and Terri could understand why. Bart's season hadn't been stellar.

"So will Anita be able to keep Bart and Alyssa separate?" Max asked. Terri had told him that Hilton Branch's former mistress was planning on attending the race.

"I sure hope she can," Terri replied. "Bart needs to focus on driving, not on a desire to do someone bodily harm."

The air brakes gave a big *whoosh* as Terri parked the motor home and shut off the engine in the heavily guarded Drivers' and Owners' lot. Max had dressed in jeans, the first time she'd seen him in something casual. At Watkins Glen he'd been wearing khakis and a white Rocksolid broadcloth shirt.

Today the red color of his polo shirt set off his dark hair and dark-blue eyes, and the jeans hugged like a glove. All three of them would be sharing her motor home for the next two days.

"I hope Bart does well," Max said, thankfully oblivious to her sudden discomfort. It had been a long time since she'd had a man stay over, even one she wasn't planning to touch.

Terri grimaced. "So do I. My dad could use some decent finishes. My mom's been pressuring him to retire, but I know he's not ready. Yet losing gets really depressing."

"I can understand that. I played college basketball. We made it to the Final Four. There was nothing more exciting. But I would see the players' faces on the teams we beat. Some of them knew they had no hope. It was their last chance and it was over."

"Like my racing trucks. I loved it, but I didn't have what it took to win."

"We won, but it's a glory that's long gone. Seems like a lifetime ago."

"A NASCAR season can feel that long. It can be a grueling ten months when you aren't winning. My dad said that the worst part of these last few weeks has been that everyone seems more focused on what's in Alyssa's tell-all book than on racing. He said everyone's been trying to get advance copies so they can know what's actually inside. Even I have to admit a morbid fascination with her."

"Perhaps it's like watching a train wreck," Max theorized.

Mandy stood, stretched and moved to the front. "So we're finally here, right? We get to go outside and look around?"

It amazed Terri how much Mandy looked like her dad, especially in hair and eye color.

"Yep. We're here. I need to take your dad to the credentials trailer and get him signed in. You're too young to have a pass, but as long as you're with one of us, you'll be good to go. I think PDQ has a T-shirt for you to wear. Either Anita or my dad will have it and we'll see them soon. I'm not exactly sure how this works. I've never brought anyone under eighteen, but the drivers have their kids here all the time."

"I would hate for them to throw me out when I'm kind of already inside the fence," Mandy said.

"Exactly," Terri replied with a light laugh. She liked Max's daughter, even if she wasn't exactly comfortable being around her. Terri remembered what it was like being a kid, but unlike Mandy, Terri had been off racing every weekend, starting with go-carts and working her way up to cars the moment she was licensed to drive.

"How about I introduce you to some of the drivers' kids?" Terri suggested. Now that was something she could do. "It all depends on who's here this weekend, but I think you'll really like everyone. Since Bristol's not too far away, a bunch of people may fly in tomorrow morning for the NASCAR Sprint Cup Series race, or they may already be here if their dad's doing double-duty and driving in the race tonight. This is usually one of the most exciting racing weekends of the season and it's pretty close to home."

"If not, it'll be the three of us all having fun," Max said, reaching over to ruffle his daughter's hair.

"Dad, stop that," Mandy said, trying to smooth the strands he'd mussed. "I'm too old for that stuff now. Whatever you do, not in public. Please."

"Sorry." He and Terri shared a sympathetic, albeit amused, glance.

Mandy didn't seem to notice the adult exchange. She was focused on the experience of being here at the race. "Lynn said this track is like a big bowl. It gets really loud, especially when all forty-three cars are on the track."

"Make sure you wear your earplugs," Terri advised.

It was almost noon when the threesome stepped out of the motor home to make their way to the infield. High chain-link fencing set off the path, and while they walked, a few people sped by on golf carts. "Got to get me one of those one of these days," Terri joked.

"That'd be nice," Mandy said.

"Mandy…" Max warned.

"It's fine," Terri said, not upset in the slightest. "You'll get used to being on your feet. We walk a lot. NASCAR advises fans to wear good shoes, because we're in the heart of the mountains. I view this as part of my workout."

They went to the credentials trailer and Max signed in. There were fans lined up outside the chain-link fence, watching and waiting to see who was entering the infield area. Terri already had her PDQ Racing hard-card credentials, and once inside they walked to where the NASCAR Sprint Cup Series haulers were parked.

Mandy was wide-eyed the moment they were infield. "I didn't realize it was all so compact," Mandy said.

"Pit road is fifty-seven feet wide, and the track and the apron are each only forty feet wide," Terri told her.

"You know all this stuff?" Mandy asked.

"My dad's a crew chief. It sinks in over the years. All this information comes into play when you're setting up a car for a given race. Cars may go faster on other tracks," Terri told her guests, "but a full lap here takes about fifteen seconds."

"Wow," Mandy said as she absorbed everything.

"Careful," Max whispered in Terri's ear. "You'll have her wanting to race cars next."

Terri smiled. "And what's wrong with that? It's exciting. People will be packed in here Saturday night. That's more people than at the NFL Super Bowl. You should hear the NASCAR fans all yell for Hart Hampton. They voted him NASCAR's most popular driver for the past two years in a row. The stands will be lined with green."

Mandy didn't respond, just turned her head and stared at everything. The haulers were less than three feet apart, and she took out her camera phone and began taking pictures of everything.

"I'm going to send some of these to Lynn," she said. "Wow! There's Kent Grosso!" Mandy snapped another shot as the reigning NASCAR Sprint Cup Series champion walked by. Kent was dressed in jeans and a T-shirt, and Terri found herself impressed that Mandy had recognized the driver. Terri had a feeling that Mandy liked racing a little more than she'd let on so far.

The roar of engines began as the NASCAR Nation-wide cars took the field for one last practice session before tonight's race. The NASCAR Sprint Cup Series cars would go out a bit later for qualifying.

"Bart should be inside since it's lunchtime," Terri said as they reached Bart's hauler. Outside, a makeshift area had been set up, and beneath a tent Bart's team worked on his car. A PDQ employee also grilled burgers, and the smell wafted to Terri's nostrils. Despite her healthy eating habits, she was a sucker for hamburgers.

"No garages?" Mandy asked. "There are some at Charlotte. I saw them when I was there for the commercial. Why not here?"

"This track is designed like the one at Charlotte," Terri answered, "but Charlotte's a mile and a half long. This one's a half mile. There's simply no room. The infield is only ten acres. My high school sat on more ground. In fact, that tunnel we walked through didn't even exist until the 1990s, thirty years after the track opened."

She walked up to a man and gave him a big smile. "Hi, Dad. How's it going?"

Philip Whalen stopped what he was doing and gave his daughter a hug. "It's going. I think the car will be perfect this weekend. If we can get a top-ten finish, I'll be happy."

"You'll get it," Terri said, studying her dad for a second. He appeared a bit tense today. At fifty-six, his hair had been gray for years, so that wasn't any indication of his stress level.

"Dad, I want you to meet Max Harper and his daughter, Mandy, my guests for the weekend," Terri said.

"Nice to meet you," Philip said, his gray eyes sizing up Max. Philip was only five foot ten.

"It's good to meet you," Max said, shaking Philip's hand. "Thank you for hosting my daughter and me."

"You're most welcome, but this is really all Terri's doing," Philip said.

"Burgers are done!" the chef called.

"Perfect timing, since we're eating lunch with you all," Terri said. "Is Bart inside?"

Philip nodded. "He has an interview this afternoon, so Anita's going over questions she knows he'll be asked. The book is coming out the Thursday before the California race, and that's all the media wants to ask him about."

"We'll get some food and eat in the lounge," Terri told Max and Mandy. Soon they had full plates and they headed inside to the front of the air-conditioned hauler. Once up some steps, they stepped into a lounge where they found Bart and Anita.

"Terri, there you are!" Bart said in greeting. "This must be the guy you were telling me about." Bart stood and shook hands with Max. "Nice to see Terri can actually date someone."

"Ha ha," Terri said. "Be good or I'll make you run extra miles this weekend."

Bart grinned. "You got me. I fear your wrath and extra miles. Ooh. Food."

Anita glanced heavenward as Bart's stomach grumbled. "Go get some lunch. We're finished, anyway."

Mandy stood and stared as Bart brushed by her. "He'll be back after he grabs a plate. He always eats inside," Terri told her young charge.

"Can I get his autograph then?" Mandy asked.

"Sure," Anita answered. "Do you need one for any of your friends?"

"Could I?" Mandy asked hesitantly.

Anita smiled. "Absolutely."

"Thank you," Mandy said, and she sat down and tried to eat. Her fingers shook a little from nerves.

"You're welcome. It's the least I can do for one of Terri's friends. I'll be back in a minute. If I don't get out there now, there might not be anything left." Anita exited the lounge.

Terri set her plate down and squeezed into the booth

next to Mandy; Max was seated on the other side. Terri leaned over and whispered just for Mandy to hear, "It's okay to relax."

Mandy leaned back over. "I can't."

"You will eventually, trust me. You're just a little starstruck."

"You mean this weird feeling goes away?" Mandy asked, her voice louder this time.

"What does?" Max asked, his forkful of baked beans poised and ready.

"This shaking feeling," Mandy said. She held up her hand. Max frowned.

"She's somewhat in awe," Terri told him. "That's natural and the drivers are used to it. Bart's an average guy underneath, so when he gets back, just talk to him like you'd talk to your dad. That'll work."

"Okay," Mandy said.

"And start eating. You'll be hungry later if you don't," Terri said.

Bart returned with a plate as full as Max's had been. Not one to eat in silence, pretty soon Bart and Max were talking about the upcoming football season and predicting how Carolina and Dallas would do. Even Anita joined in the conversation, and so did Mandy when she had something to add.

A sense of relief flowed through Terri. She'd been worried about the first meeting between Max and her friends, but all was going smoothly and everyone seemed to be getting along great. She relaxed and finished her food. Before Anita took Bart to his interview, she had him autograph a bunch of things for Mandy and even pulled out her own camera and took Bart's picture with the young girl.

"Better?" Terri said as the lounge once again contained only the three of them.

"Yes," Mandy said.

"Good, because there's still lots to do. Come on. I have to be back at the motor home later for Bart's workout, and after that we have a race to watch."

"Cool," Mandy said. Terri led the way out of the hauler, said goodbye to her dad and took them to the front-stretch pit road. NASCAR Nationwide Series practice had come to an end, and all the pit stalls were full as various teams worked on their cars.

Mandy moved a few feet ahead as they walked down pit road toward Turn Four. The entire area was a flurry of activity as team members worked at getting things ready for tonight's race.

"Thank you for this," Max said suddenly.

"Really, it's nothing. Just a peek inside my weekend world," Terri said, her eyes scanning the road ahead. Despite her deflection of his seriousness, Max's compliment had still touched her.

"Well, I appreciate you sharing this with us. It means a lot that you can be so open with me."

Max reached out and touched her hand for a second. He didn't try to hold it, and for that Terri was grateful. First, it was too soon for any public display of affection. Second, they were far too close to the pit box of the NASCAR Nationwide Series team for whom Harry worked.

Harry! Her ex-fiancé. How could she have forgotten that he'd be here?

Suddenly a familiar voice said, "Hi, Terri. How are you?"

Oh, crap.

CHAPTER TEN

TERRI TURNED, facing the man she'd loved and dated for two years. She'd worn his ring for a few months until the commitment had simply scared her off. While he'd moved on and supposedly was dating someone else, the ending hadn't been pleasant for either. She'd seen him almost daily until he'd gotten a job with another team.

"Hi, Harry," Terri said. Mandy was about twelve feet ahead, so she couldn't hear the exchange. Max, however, was right at Terri's side, taking in everything.

The ensuing pause was barely a second, but the silence stretched awkwardly. "Harry, this is my friend Max Harper. Max, this is Harry, my—"

"Former fiancé," Harry supplied helpfully, shaking Max's hand. "Not that I'm any competition. I'm getting married in November."

"That's wonderful," Terri said. She honestly was happy for Harry and prayed that came through in her tone.

"Yeah," Harry said, his eyes getting a bit dreamy for a moment before he blinked away an obvious surge of feelings for his girlfriend. "I haven't seen you in a while but wanted to tell you myself when I did. The word's not out yet that Sue and I are engaged, but it will be soon."

"I heard you were seeing someone."

"Yep and we're very happy." Harry shifted his weight from one foot to the other. He glanced at Max but kept his focus on Terri. "I was a bit…unpleasant there at the end, and I want to apologize for that. I was a bear."

"Thank you, but we both probably were," Terri said.

She glanced at Max. Once they'd left the hauler, he'd donned sunglasses. They made him sexy as all get-out, yet at the same time hid the emotion in his eyes. She knew he felt *some*thing, for the corner of his mouth had an almost imperceptible twitch as he observed the exchange.

Harry coughed a little. "I gotta get back to work," he said. "Good to see you again, Terri." He nodded at Max. "Nice to meet you."

"The same," Max said. He stepped forward to follow Terri who'd covered the distance to where Mandy waited.

"Who was that?" Mandy asked.

"A friend. He's a front tire changer," Terri told her. "He worked for my dad a long time ago. You'll see him work for his current team tonight."

"Oh," Mandy said, her curiosity apparently satisfied.

Max, however, was a different story. Terri could feel the tension emanating from him. It was as tangible as the heat rising from the pavement.

"So do you have any other *friends?*" he asked as they continued along pit road.

"Not in the way you're insinuating," Terri said, bristling slightly. "We dated for two years and were engaged before I called it off. I didn't come out like a bubble, you know. Like you, I have a history."

"It caught me off guard, that's all. I only wish you'd told me about Harry so I wouldn't have been so surprised."

"Now is not the place to discuss this," she said. Pit road was loud. Talking to someone meant shouting, or leaning so close that your lips were practically to the person's ear.

The last thing Terri wanted was to give anyone a reason to gossip. Already tongues would be wagging that she'd brought someone to the track—a guy with a kid, at that. The only guests she ever brought were her girlfriends.

"Oh, God," she said, gazing forward.

"What?" Max asked.

Despite the heat, Terri shuddered. She and Max could talk about their pasts later. "That's her in the flesh."

Up ahead, Alyssa Ritchie and her entourage were coming down pit road. She was impossible to miss. Five-eight with bleached-blond hair, Alyssa wore tight designer jeans and a top that showed off to the fullest her obvious breast augmentation.

"I thought they had a dress code," Max said.

Terri eyed the low-cut top and the three-inch heels. "Unfortunately it's not specific enough to keep out tramps."

"Why is she here?" Max asked. "Her book's not out yet."

"She finally got her team sponsorship. She tried to sponsor Will Branch for a while, if you can believe it, but thankfully that didn't happen. Instead, she hooked up with team owner Larry Preston, and she's sponsoring Brad Stewart. No one wants her here, but she's bought her way in."

Mandy was staring at Alyssa.

"Don't gape," Max said. "I know what you're thinking. You thought your mom could be over the top sometimes, but this woman…"

"…takes the cake," Mandy finished, her expression one of classic horror. Alyssa wore huge sunglasses and didn't even turn her head as she simply walked forward, making the crowd in front of her part.

"So, what's on the hood of Brad Stewart's car?" Max asked.

"I don't know," Terri replied. "She's using his car to promote a brand of diet products called Slim Like Me. It's so irritating! Even if I wasn't fit already, I sure wouldn't use any of that stuff or buy her self-help book. I think the book cover is what's on the hood, but I'm not certain. Poor Brad Stewart. He's driving around the track promoting the devil."

"There certainly is a lot of drama in this sport," Max commented. "Rocksolid's praying Billy Budd's as squeaky clean as he comes off."

"He's pretty mild-mannered, but I think there's drama in just about every sport. Didn't you have drama in your college basketball days? Especially the championships?"

Max thought for a moment. "Yeah, guess so. The event lasted a month and the arenas were packed."

"I bet there's drama at your office, too."

He shook his head. "Um, not that much. I have to say, Rocksolid's a great place to work. There's the occasional upset, but for the most part, the company is, well, to make a bad pun, Rocksolid. It's invested wisely and hasn't suffered when paying out for things like hurricanes. Some companies really saw their bottom lines plummet, which scared investors."

"Dad, work talk's boring," Mandy scolded her father as she stopped to get a race card from a holder. "We're here to have fun, not talk about insurance." She rolled her eyes at Terri. "You have to stop him or he'll go on forever. He's a fun sucker."

"Am not, and I agree, no more work talk since we are here for fun," Max said. Terri smiled as she caught Max check his arm movement—he'd been about to ruffle his daughter's hair.

They explored the entire infield, watching part of the qualifying from the top of Bart's hauler, where they had a 360-degree view of the track. Then they made their way back to the motor home so that Terri could give Bart a workout. Max and Mandy used the time to peruse merchandise row, where various team haulers sold everything from T-shirts to books.

"So how's it going so far?" Bart asked Terri once he was certain Max and Mandy were out of earshot.

"Good," Terri replied. She mainly wanted him to run and do some cardio. She adjusted the grade on the treadmill, a staple in her workout routine.

"Just good?" Bart asked with an arch of a blond eyebrow. "The guy seemed pretty into you."

"That was before we ran into Harry."

"Ohh." Bart winced. Terri was pleased to note that after ten minutes at a six-point-five speed and a grade of two he was hardly winded. He'd really increased his endurance. When she'd started, he'd barely lasted five minutes at five miles an hour and no grade. "I bet that meeting went well."

"Did you hear Harry's getting married?" Terri asked.

"He is?" Bart's shock lasted a second. "Huh. That should help you out."

"It's not like Harry and I haven't been civil. It's been a few years since we were engaged. He did let Max know he was my ex-fiancé, right before he apologized for some of the silliness we'd endured at the end."

"As long as he's happy," Bart said. He remained silent for a minute, as his elevated heart rate made speaking more difficult.

"He looked good," Terri said. She sighed. "I was a different person then, you know?"

"You sure about that?" Bart asked.

"No, which is the problem. The only commitment I've really made is to my career and to following the race schedule. Max…he's one of those serious types. Maybe having a kid makes you like that. Okay, enough talking about me. You're supposed to be concentrating, not dwelling on my little dramas. You only have a few minutes left before we do some hand weights."

"Heck, listening to you keeps my mind off my issues. It's nice to know I'm not the only one whose life can best be described as a big fat mess."

"Yeah, at least if you're going to have a pity party you don't have to be alone. Now focus," Terri told him.

"I just figure everyone has problems. Mine have been major, but I've decided everyone has issues and what might be trivial to me could be really significant to them and vice versa. It's all about perspective."

Terri tilted her head and stared at him. "That's quite profound. What have you done with the real Bart

Branch? You're not Will pretending to be him, are you? I know you used to do that when you were kids."

"Will wouldn't be stupid enough to get on this treadmill and huff and puff for you," Bart said as Terri lowered his speed, allowing him to cool down.

"Yeah, but you could probably outrun Will if you needed to," Terri said.

Bart grinned at the idea. "That could come in handy someday."

Terri chuckled. "Knowing you two, it probably will."

"So, you going to talk to Max about Harry tonight?"

"I guess so," Terri said, depressed at the prospect. "I didn't even think about mentioning Harry before. I guess I should have."

Bart reached for a water bottle and took a quick sip. "Good luck," he said.

Terri had a feeling she'd need it.

"THIS IS SO COOL," Mandy said. She and her dad were walking down merchandise row, where hauler after hauler was opened on one side to reveal all sorts of items for purchase. One could find everything from stickers costing about a dollar to one-hundred-dollar collectibles. If you wanted it, the haulers sold it.

A few of the big drivers, like Hart Hampton, had their own merchandise trailers. Others relied on their race shop trailer to sell their wares. For example, PDQ racing had a trailer that sold Bart Branch gear and also that of other drivers in the PDQ stable.

"I need to get Lynn something that has Will Branch on it," Mandy said, and after surveying all the trailers,

Max and Mandy returned to the Taney Motorsports hauler, where Max took out his credit card and bought Mandy's friend a T-shirt and a key chain. Then it was off to the PDQ trailer, where he exercised his charge card again.

"Thanks, Dad," Mandy said as she clutched two plastic shopping bags.

"So now you're into this racing stuff?" Max asked as they walked up to a food stand. While they'd eat dinner later with Terri, some popcorn and soda sounded like an ideal snack to tide them over.

He also wanted to rent Mandy a race scanner and headset, something that Alan Henson had suggested would help Mandy enjoy the race.

Henson attended at least six races a year and had advised Max that, unless you were in a suite with a television set going, you often didn't know what was going on, as the track didn't broadcast play-by-play over an audio system. It also didn't have a big scoreboard, like at a professional baseball, football or hockey game. The track relied on a scoring pylon, where whoever's car number was up top was the race leader.

"I think I like this," Mandy said as she took a sip of her soda.

"What—being here?"

"Everything. I think Terri's pretty cool and she knows everyone. She's fun. I can't believe I got Bart's autograph and she's going to get Will's for Lynn. Can I call Lynn?"

"Sure," Max said. His daughter balanced her snack food and drink as she retrieved her cell phone. "You're going to call her now?"

"Why not? I already sent her some pictures."

Max glanced to his right, watching some people line up for a racing simulator similar to the one Rocksolid had used last weekend. This time it was another driver's number and sponsor decals on the car. He gave a wry grin. His daughter's world had expanded and he was no longer her number-one focus. As she talked to Lynn, her voice was excited as she relayed the day's events.

He strolled along, following Mandy, who like many teenagers, had mastered the art of walking and talking. He'd watched races on television, seen Watkins Glen in person, but this one had a different feel to it, aside from the credentials holder he wore around his neck.

Maybe it was the intimate size of the track—that many people in such a small space intensified everything. People were making a weekend of the events and the place hummed with energy. He checked his watch. Terri should be about finished with Bart. He hadn't wanted to get in her way.

He sighed, still somewhat rattled to find out she'd been engaged once. Not that Terri didn't have the right to a relationship or a past, he thought. He wasn't jealous but more surprised that someone who claimed to be footloose and fancy-free had been almost ready to settle down. Had he not met Harry face-to-face, he never would have guessed Terri had once been considering a trip down the aisle.

That fact proved he still didn't know her as well as he thought he did. Like the first time he'd heard her voice, he'd misjudged her.

He also worried that should anything develop

between them—and he did feel a very strong connection to her—there was no promise that she wouldn't up and bolt one day.

He'd had that happen already with Lola. She'd done quite a number on him, and one thing was for certain—he never wanted to go through that again.

"THAT WAS SO GREAT!" Mandy said later that night as they walked back to Terri's motor home after the end of the NASCAR Nationwide Series race. Although Mandy didn't follow any of the drivers in that particular series, many of the NASCAR Sprint Cup Series drivers had participated, and the race had been a nail-biter. The time separating the first- and second-place finishers had been less than a second.

Mandy stifled a yawn and Terri shifted the strap of the fourteen-inch cooler they'd carried inside onto her other shoulder. "I can carry that," Max volunteered.

"It's empty now," Terri told him. Earlier it had held some snacks, three sodas and some bottled water. Each person could carry in a cooler, but they'd only brought one between them.

She flashed her credentials and the guard let them through another security gate. "All I know is that I'm tired. What about you?"

Mandy yawned again in response to Terri's question.

"You'll sleep soundly tonight," Max predicted with a laugh.

Mandy would sleep on the chair that converted to a single bed, while Max would use the sofa that folded out into a queen bed.

They were all sharing the bathroom—the tiniest space in the motor home. It took a few minutes to transform the living area, but once done there was very little walking space. She stood in the kitchen and waited for Mandy to finish in the bathroom. If it had been just her and a girlfriend, Terri would have had no issue with brushing her teeth in the kitchen sink. However, no way was she doing any personal grooming in front of Max.

"Thanks again," Max told her. He smiled and took a sip of the water bottle she'd handed him once they'd gotten back. Terri's credo was keep hydrated, especially when in the mountains of eastern Tennessee.

"You don't have to keep thanking me," she said. "I'm having fun sharing this weekend with you."

"I'd like to talk to you if we can have some alone time," Max said.

"If you're not uncomfortable talking in my bedroom, you could come there once Mandy's asleep. I promise you, all we'll do is talk."

His expression was sheepish. "Which is all I was expecting."

About forty minutes later she heard a light knock on her door and Max entered. He'd changed into a T-shirt and floor-length pajama bottoms, both totally respectable.

"That's your spot," Terri said, pointing to the foot of her bed where the edge touched the wall. Her bed sat against the back and a side wall of the motor home. The mattress dipped as Max sat.

"Be sure to watch your head when you stand up," she told him, gesturing to the cabinets overhead.

"Every inch of space is utilized in these things, isn't it?" he asked.

Terri tucked her hair behind her ear. "Yeah. I remember when I first bought this unit. I'd had a smaller version, but stepping up to driving a motor home is a huge deal. This particular one had been out with a country-music singer for a year-long tour. I couldn't afford a brand-new one—they're ridiculously expensive—and the company I bought this from totally refurbished the interior before I took possession. New furniture, bedding, carpet, everything. The engine's diesel and should last forever, with proper maintenance. I'm not one who can buy a new motor home every year." She stopped, afraid she was babbling. Ever since running into Harry, she'd been nervous around Max.

"So how long have you been traveling?" Max asked.

"You mean besides all my life?" Terri said.

He seemed surprised. "Really?"

She fingered the edge of the comforter. "Pretty much. Once I could race I traveled. I love being on the road for part of the year. Even now I can't give it up."

"It has to be great seeing the country. I got to do some of that during college. We tried to do some sightseeing in the cities where we played."

"Then you understand."

He nodded. "I do. I think you're lucky. Mandy and I don't get to vacation as much as we'd like. Maybe after this year. Seeing the actual place is always so much better than reading about it in books or magazines."

"I don't go to all the races anymore—I think I told you that. But I like the freedom that this motor home represents. I drove it to the Grand Canyon last December. A lot of car companies will come to where you are and pick you up. So it's pretty easy to get some wheels once I reach my destination."

"I guess I've been more tied down. I've been living in the same house since Mandy was born."

"Technically, so have I. That is, I've been in the same house where I was born if you discount the fact that I moved from the main house to the guest cottage out back. And let me tell you, that sounds like it's fancy, but it's not. This motor home is larger."

"You don't need much room, though, if you're never there," Max pointed out.

"True," Terri agreed. "I rent a small studio in town that doubles as my office, and it's not too far from my dad's shop."

"You're really close to your dad."

She sensed Max hoped that he and Mandy would be the same once she was older. "We *are* close. I watch out for him when I'm at the track. My mom wants him to retire, but I think my dad would hate it. He's not the type to sit around and fish every day, and he sure loves to fish."

"I like to fish but never have the time," Max said with a sigh. "This Rising Stars Program takes every minute. But it's like saving for a big trip. The result will be worth it. I've just got to grin and bear it for a year."

"Which is admirable. And you shouldn't be worried. You've gone a great job raising Mandy. She's very proud of you, I can tell," Terri said.

"Thanks. It hasn't been easy."

"Is anything we want easy?" Terri leaned back

136   TAILSPIN

against her pillow. She'd stretched her legs out under the covers and her feet were a few inches from Max.

"No, I don't think so. If it was, we probably wouldn't appreciate it as much. It's like kids who get those toys they clamor for. The toys end up being forgotten in a week."

"You're right about that. I bought one of my nephews the video game he wanted for Christmas. He played it for about two days and then the next time I saw him I asked him how he liked it, he told me he'd beaten it and given it to a friend."

"Great," Max said.

"Yeah." Terri nodded. "Once he'd won, it was old news. He's a kid. They don't come with instructions."

"You're relating really well to Mandy. She likes you."

"Does she?" Terri found herself pleased. "I like her, too. I'll admit to being nervous. I'm not used to kids. My niece and nephews, yes, but..."

"You're doing fine," Max reassured her. "Mandy's resilient since Lola puts her in the middle a lot. Mandy loves her mother, but she's learned that Lola's more interested in what Lola wants. You've paid genuine attention to Mandy. She respects how you treat her."

"Thanks. I'm glad I haven't struck out already."

"I doubt that'll happen," Max said with a smile.

Terri sat there a second and then asked the question that had been on her mind. "So how did you meet Lola? If you don't mind telling me."

"College. We met in a bar after my team had won an important game. She was the most beautiful woman in the room, and out of all the guys she had to choose from, she wanted me."

He laughed sadly. "Sounds great, doesn't it? It wasn't. What probably should have stayed a one-night stand turned into something else. My teammates thought I was really lucky, and I didn't have the maturity to realize how self-destructive our relationship was. By the time I figured it out, she turned up pregnant and that was that. On the bright side, though, I got Mandy."

Terri shifted. "That's a great way to look at things."

"She's the best thing that ever happened to me. I'd never trade my daughter for a different past."

Terri was impressed with his frankness. "When I look back," she said, "I wish I'd been brave enough to break up with Harry earlier. I knew things weren't right between us. Why is it that people think getting married will fix things?"

"I don't know," Max said.

"Deep down I knew I wasn't supposed to marry Harry. But I was afraid. I know many people who have stayed in relationships because they're afraid of what's on the other side, which is that there isn't anyone there for them. It's the fear of being alone."

Terri paused and leaned back against her pillow. She was oddly comfortable talking to Max, even more so than she was with Pam and Libby. She could tell them anything, but she'd never begin to tell them things like this. With Max it seemed as natural as breathing.

"The truth is, if I'd stayed with Harry, I probably wouldn't be where I am now. He never wanted me to pursue my commercial work or training other drivers. He was a bit jealous and possessive. He worried constantly and I felt he couldn't trust me. I wasn't unfaithful. But like a doctor, I do have to touch someone's body to get the job done. But that's all it is. A job."

"I don't have a problem with you doing any of that," Max said.

"I think I hear a *but* coming," Terri said, studying his face.

"You could be a serious complication to my life. I haven't let anyone in for a long time. And I can't get into a relationship with you unless I know it's serious. At the same time, I don't know if I'm ready for a relationship. I don't know if I'll ever get married again. For ten years remarrying has been the furthest thing from my mind."

"I don't know if I'll ever be ready," Terri said.

"So what do we do? Touching you dominates my thoughts. But I don't want casual. I can't promise forever, either."

"As if there are any guarantees of that," Terri said.

He sighed. "I know. And I'm not afraid of being alone. I've been alone since Lola."

"You're not alone. You have Mandy. You have purpose, that higher calling of being a parent. I envy you for that. Not that I want to be a mother in the next minute. But I'm single and I'm career-focused. That's it. Against you, I look selfish and more like someone who can't find a guy, rather than someone who chooses to wait for true love."

"I'm not afraid to wait or of never dating anyone again and being some workaholic bachelor for the rest of my days. I've mastered that. But you've thrown a monkey wrench into the cogs of my life. I want to touch you. I want to kiss you everywhere. When I married Lola

I thought we'd be together for better or worse. It was always worse, but it still stings when someone leaves."

"I can relate to that. How about we promise each other we'll be exclusive for as long as we're together? We'll also tell each other everything."

"I can live with no secrets. But if we get close, there's no guarantee you'll stay."

"You said you can't offer any guarantee of forever, either. Who's to say you won't leave me?"

Max shook his head. "I don't know."

The relationship with his ex must have scarred Max deeply. This was why Terri never dated divorced men. She mentally kicked herself, but she still didn't want to stop seeing him.

"You've upset my world, too," she admitted. "I want to be with you. I never bring guys to the race track. This is my world and I'm careful about who I share it with."

"You shared it with Harry," Max said.

"Yes, but Harry works in this world, too, and maybe that was part of his initial appeal. He fit into my lifestyle. We could travel together. Also, my brother had settled down, gotten married and had a son. My mother kept on at me that maybe I should be doing the same. Mom's very traditional. I love her dearly, but she's never worked outside the home and I don't think she understands my career aspirations. Anyway, suddenly Harry wanted me to stay home, do the same things his mother and my mother did. And that's not me."

"You felt smothered."

He seemed to understand and she was grateful. "Precisely. It had nothing to do with not being able to love him, but rather with not being able to love myself. I'd lost part of me, a part that was important to who I was. The more I tried to change things, the worse it got. Finally the stress of pretending became too great. I called the whole wedding off."

"And so life was better?" Max asked.

She shook her head. "Not even close. The next year was hell. Harry worked for my dad. Harry's a great guy and a lot of people couldn't understand why I'd broken things off with him. They considered him my perfect match."

"I think everyone in my family breathed a sigh of relief when Lola and I were finished," Max admitted.

She nodded. "I just knew being with Harry for the rest of my life was wrong. Being alone can be frightening, but I'm a firm believer that things happen the way they do for a reason."

"Even your truck?" Max asked with a smile.

"I guess fate meant for you and me to meet," Terri conceded. She longed to edge closer to him, to kiss him as she had after their dinner date. They'd put a lot of cards on the table tonight. "You being in my life is important to me."

His grin faded. "It scares you."

"No. Yes. Because my liking you and caring about you gives you the power to hurt me. I swore I'd never let myself be hurt again. Although I broke things off with Harry, the situation afterward was painful. I don't want to go through that again. Which is, I guess, about the same thing you were telling me earlier about you and Lola."

"In chess this would be considered a stalemate. We have each other checked. No one's going to win this."

"I don't see how," she said in resigned agreement.

Max shifted, then moved closer. "That means we both have to move at the same time."

"That's not in the rules," she protested as his face came closer to hers.

"In this case I think we're going to have to write our own playbook," Max said.

He was mere inches from her, his breath minty fresh from the toothpaste he'd brushed with.

"Each of us is risking something here. It's like a big vicious circle. We simply each need to step inside and get off the roundabout."

"You have the oddest sayings," she told him. "But they make sense."

"Good, because I'm not exactly a wordsmith. I'm just hoping they do the trick, unlike with Mandy who says my statements are lame. I like you, Terri. A lot. There's something here between us, and as much as it scares me—and I'm man enough to admit that—I'd be a fool to let you walk out of my life. I'll risk it if you will."

"You—" she began.

He silenced her by balancing on one arm and lifting the other, placing his forefinger on her lips. "Shh. Let's at least give ourselves this one taste. You've been tempting me all day."

She'd dreamed of kissing him again, and then her dream was reality as his lips found hers. Terri found herself swept away. The physical connection that had been humming between them hadn't diminished.

Instead, it flared to life, proving that what she'd felt hadn't been a fluke. His touch was tender yet insistent, and she let herself forget everything but the response his body called from hers.

They were both breathing heavily when they parted ten minutes later. "As much as I'd like to continue this, we'd better stop here," Max told her, his fingers stroking her chin.

"Probably wise," Terri agreed. If not, they'd get even more carried away. Their kissing had done nothing to quench the fire burning between them. If anything, their need for each other had grown stronger. Terri knew that making love with Max Harper was inevitable, and that when it occurred it would be incredible. But tonight, with Mandy just down the hall, was not the time. She also wanted to get to know him better, get them on more solid footing if they were to be a couple, especially taking everything one day at a time with no long-term plans.

Max stroked her face again, and then he gave her one last kiss before he left for the sofa bed.

She watched as the lights down the hall flickered out, listened as the sofa creaked with Max's weight. His kiss had washed away her doubts, at least for the moment. She felt invincible, like she could handle anything, even uncertainty. She'd never felt like this before—that an unknown future with a man wasn't to be feared, but embraced.

Terri closed her eyes and touched her smiling lips once before sleep claimed her.

CHAPTER ELEVEN

THE WEEKEND was a success all around. And despite Alyssa's presence at the track, Bart had placed ninth, a solid top-ten finish that had had her father beaming. Bart's brother, Will, had taken third. Reigning NASCAR Sprint Cup Series champion Kent Grosso had brought home another win, and he was in good shape heading into the final races before the Chase for the NASCAR Sprint Cup.

Of course, everything went wrong the moment Terri pulled up in front of Max's house. She should have been prepared. Her life never ran that smoothly.

"What's Mom doing here?" Mandy asked as Terri's motor home's air brakes *whooshed.*

"I have no idea," Max said, and Terri could tell he wasn't too pleased to see his ex's car parked in the driveway.

"Is she inside?" Terri asked, not seeing anyone waiting in the car or sitting on Max's porch.

"She doesn't have a key," Max said. He glanced at Mandy. "You didn't give her one, did you?"

"No." Mandy shook her head.

At that moment Lola came out from around the back

of the house. Mandy, Max and Terri had spent Saturday night in Bristol, getting up and heading home early that morning. It wasn't even eleven. Most churches weren't finished with services. Terri opened the door and Max stepped out onto the pavement.

"There you are," Lola greeted with a wide welcoming smile. "I thought you'd be back already, and so I came to take Mandy out shopping."

The hackles on Terri's back rose at Lola's syrupy tone. Men were often blind to a woman like Lola's wiles and subterfuge. But another woman could always see them. To Terri, Lola was as readable as a book—and Terri didn't like what she was reading. The thought hit her that Lola and Alyssa Ritchie would probably make great friends, except that they'd be constantly trying to outshine each other.

"Hi, Mom," Mandy said, climbing out of the motor home.

"Hi, darling," Lola greeted, giving her daughter an air kiss to her cheek. Terri used the exchange to study Max's ex-wife. Whereas Alyssa was blond, Lola matched Max in hair color. Terri could understand Max's attraction all those years ago.

"You coming out?" Max called, stepping back onto the first rung of the motor home.

"Should I?" Terri asked him.

"You might as well meet Lola. I would have preferred to have arranged the meeting on my terms but…" He stood there uneasily.

"Don't worry, it takes a lot to scare me away," Terri reassured him.

Lola appeared to be only half-listening to Mandy's recitation of the weekend's events, and she turned as Terri and Max exited. "You must be Terri."

"I am," Terri said, giving Lola a friendly smile.

Lola's own smile didn't reach her eyes and her handshake felt like a limp fish. The two women were only inches apart, with the height advantage to Lola. But Terri trained big men. Size didn't intimidate her. Attitude and personality were what impressed her, and so far Lola hadn't done anything worth notice.

"Well, it's nice to meet you," Lola said. "Thank you for inviting them. You must be tired from the drive. Please don't stay on our account."

"Oh, I'm fine," Terri replied, not surprised to see an irritated flicker in Lola's eyes before they narrowed.

"Max, go get Mandy's suitcase," Lola said. As Max returned to the motor home, Lola continued, "She starts school soon and she really needs some new things. Max doesn't have any fashion sense, not for a girl her age. I know what all the style rages are. It's a woman's touch Mandy needs." She gave Terri a conspiratorial wink that hinted at something more. "Men."

Terri simply nodded, not voicing her opinion. Mandy's clothes were fine. Mandy had disappeared into the motor home and she returned with her shopping bags and her suitcase.

"You should see all the autographs I got!" she told her mom. "Terri knows everyone and I even have a bunch for Lynn. I told her I might be able to go see her today. I'll unlock the door, Dad."

"This is my custody weekend with my daughter,"

Max reminded his ex-wife as Mandy stepped out of earshot. "You shouldn't spring surprises like this and arrive unannounced."

Lola planted her hands on her hips, waited for Mandy to go into the house before turning on Terri and Max. "It's important that she spend time with me and this is the only time I have."

"You could have waited until next weekend," Max said.

"I don't know if I'll be here next weekend," Lola replied.

Terri knew Max could fight his own battles, and this one was beginning to brew. "I've got to get going," she said. "My brother's coming for dinner at my parents' and I can't wait to see my niece and nephews."

"I thought we'd talk and—" Max began.

But Terri stepped back into the motor home and shook her head. "Call me later."

"Okay," Max said. He didn't appear too happy. He turned to face Lola as Terri drove off.

MAX FROWNED as he watched the motor home move off down the street.

"You really need to be more discreet," Lola said, her disdain obvious. "Mandy could be hurt."

"Good grief," Max replied. "Since when did you start caring about your daughter? You leave her for months and years at a time. You've always treated her as an afterthought. Don't try to sell me on your motherly devotion now."

"Is that what you're looking for with Terri?" Lola jerked a thumb in the direction the motor home disappeared. "You just met her. You're always Mr. Safe-and-Secure. I can't believe you went away for the weekend with someone you hardly know."

Max widened his stance and crossed his arms. "I like her. We had a great time."

"Oh, please," Lola said, displaying her drama-queen side. "Mark my words, you are making a big mistake."

The front door slammed and Mandy reappeared. "I'm ready," she told her parents.

"Get in the car, darling," Lola said, her voice composed and controlled as she made nice in front of their daughter. She waited until Mandy had climbed inside. "You and I will talk tonight," she told Max, and then she was gone, her tires squealing as she drove off a tad too fast.

Max reached for the luggage sitting on the curb. First he waved at his neighbor, who was out watering her flowers. Then he went inside and heaved a great sigh. Lola could be extremely nasty. He wished she could find whatever she was searching for.

He'd thought she was settled this last time, as she was living with some big-shot producer, but then, like a bad penny, she turned up in Charlotte again. He hated that Terri had witnessed even part of Lola's theatrics and hoped it hadn't scared her away.

TERRI ARRIVED HOME and parked her motor home in her dad's garage. Next weekend the races were in California, much too far for her to drive.

She tossed her suitcase on her bed and glanced around her small cottage. Basically she had two rooms.

When her grandfather had inherited the land, he'd built the main house where her parents now lived. Her dad had used the guest cottage as an office, and now she inhabited the space.

Her dad's vehicle had been in the driveway when she'd driven up. He'd traveled home last night and she'd go over to the main house once she unpacked.

Terri knew she was fortunate. She'd grown up with two parents who loved her dearly. She had what fifty percent of the population didn't—a traditional Ozzie-and-Harriet family structure.

Her phone rang and she picked it up. "Hi, Mom."

"Hi, honey. I'm just making sure you're home and that you'll be coming over. We'll be eating at five."

"I'll be there," Terri replied, and after unpacking, taking a short nap and freshening up, Terri walked the 250 feet to the main house.

She stepped inside a few minutes before five, immediately inhaling the scents of dinner. Her mother was making a roast and the entire house smelled delicious.

"Hi, honey. Zack's running a few minutes late," Terri's mom greeted her. Louise wiped her hands on her apron before giving her daughter a big hug. "So what's new with you?"

"Tons," Terri replied, settling herself on one of the center island's stools. She proceeded to tell her mom about Max and Mandy and their weekend at Bristol.

"It's a shame about his ex-wife," her mom commented. "Some women just don't know when to let go."

"You didn't have any problems, right? You married Dad out of high school."

"Yes. We knew we were meant to be together sophomore year. But I had friends. Some of them weren't so lucky. And your aunt Suzanne is on husband number five."

"True." Terri acknowledged that fact with a tilt of her head. "So how do you know? I mean, obviously I thought I was in love with Harry, but as we got closer to the wedding, I knew it was all wrong."

"People often confuse passion for true love. True love takes patience and persistence."

"Okay, you lost me there," Terri admitted.

Her mom began retrieving serving dishes. "Love is a choice. It takes a lot of persistence and tenacity to hang in there when things don't go right. Passion can be fleeting. It's hot and heavy. Fantastic. But passion doesn't fill you up. You feel empty afterward."

"That makes sense."

"I'm not saying love can't be passionate, but true love means hard work. You and the person you love are willing to set aside your own goals and dreams because you've put the other person's needs ahead of your own. And you do it willingly, not because he asks you. You realize your goals and dreams have changed to include that person. If all you have is passion, you'll feel resentful, instead of giving."

"Harry wanted me to stay home and give up stuff."

"And that's why you weren't meant for each other. If you'd really loved him deep down, you'd have gladly done what he'd wanted. The fact that you didn't want to and it caused conflict between you meant that you two weren't meant to be. You were in love, but it wasn't the kind of love that stands the test of time."

"You make it sound so simple. Surely you and Dad fight."

She shook her head. "Not really. I would describe it as negotiating. We've been together far too long for silliness. He's the love of my life and my best friend. I knew he'd be on the road most of his life, but that's part of him. He'd be unhappy not doing what he does."

"Hmm." Terri mulled over what her mom said. There was a difference between being in love and truly loving someone, flaws and all.

"I probably haven't helped much," her mom acknowledged as she removed the standing-rib roast from the oven.

"Yes, you have. I've never dated someone who's been married before. I steered away from that type of guy."

"Well, maybe you should go on a few more dates with him. What can it hurt?"

"Perhaps my heart?"

"True. But if you're not willing to put your heart out there in the first place, you won't find what you're looking for."

"Dating sucks," Terri proclaimed.

"Everything worth having comes with a lot of hard work," her mom said.

"That's Dad's saying," Terri protested.

Her mom grinned. "Nope, it's mine. I let him borrow it."

They laughed, and then Zack and Miranda arrived with Jesse, Julie and Jake. Terri hugged her nephews and niece, and then ushered them off into the family room where she and her young charges performed as band members to an interactive video game.

"You're pretty good at this, Aunt Terri," Jesse said. He played guitar to Terri's bass.

Then it was dinnertime, and later Zack and his family said their goodbyes and headed home. Terri stayed behind to help her mother clean up before making her way back to her cottage.

She turned on the television set, the sound filling the room. She'd dropped Max off this morning without any type of plan to see each other again. She frowned. She knew that a budding romance needed work, but as she sat on her couch she decided what was bothering her was that so far she'd made all the moves. She'd asked him to dinner. She'd asked him to Bristol. She couldn't keep being the one doing the chasing.

Even if it meant she'd lose him.

MAX'S SUNDAY NIGHT alone time ended when Lola brought Mandy home around eight o'clock. Mandy, loaded down with shopping bags, disappeared immediately into her room, giving Lola the opening Lola had been waiting for.

"We need to talk," Lola reminded him. She was standing in his office doorway.

"About what?" Max asked. He'd been in the middle of reviewing an advertising-expenditure proposal and he turned around in his swivel chair to face his ex-wife.

"I'm concerned about Mandy," Lola said, entering the room.

"*Now* why?" Max said. He knew his voice sounded harsh, but with Lola it was always something. He struggled to maintain civility and he usually succeeded, but tonight…well, after this morning, his irritation remained.

"Max, I am not your enemy," Lola said, sensing his mood. She moved closer, her perfume wafting to his nostrils. She must have sprayed on her signature scent before coming into the house.

He shifted and then stood so he could move around and put distance between them if need be. Lola had her "I'm on a mission" face. She'd turned bewitching and beguiling, a sure sign she wanted something from him.

"Max, I think we need to be on the same page. Mandy needs *both* her parents in her life. I know I've been remiss at times, but I was misguided. We all make mistakes, don't we? Isn't the key thing forgiveness? Shouldn't you be more understanding? Am I wrong in thinking this way and asking that of you?"

All the years of dealing with Lola and her various issues had turned Max into a cynic where she was concerned. Still, perhaps he should give her the benefit of the doubt. He could at least hear her out.

"Forgiveness is always a good policy," he said.

She beamed at him. "Exactly. Even your company forgives the first little fender bender. Don't you think you could do the same where I'm concerned? I'm not a bad person."

"No, you're not." He could at least say those words and not be lying. "But you've done some terrible things."

She nodded and appeared both guilty and contrite. "I know. I'm so sorry. I never intended to hurt you or Mandy. I was lost. I was trying to find myself. I did so at your expense. But I've changed."

She seemed earnest, but Max wasn't able to completely set aside his skepticism. His ex had fooled him too many times before. She always had an ace up her sleeve or an escape clause.

"I'd like to believe that," he said.

"I *have* changed," Lola insisted. She moved closer, giving him an excellent view of her cleavage.

"I'm glad you've changed," Max said, shifting his gaze away from Lola and the charms she was trying to showcase.

"Are you?" Lola asked. She smiled tentatively. "Did you ever ask yourself why I keep coming back to Charlotte, instead of just staying in L.A.?"

"Because you have a daughter here who loves you?"

Lola's smile widened. "Don't be so modest. Of course she's part of it. But I also come back because of you."

He couldn't help himself. He snorted. "Lola, please."

She pouted. "No, I mean it. Don't you know how I feel about you? You are the best man on the planet. No one has ever come close to you." She trembled a little. "No one."

Max felt his stomach sink as he wrestled for control. When she'd first left him, he would have killed to hear her utter those words and mean them.

Now her declaration was a little too late. He'd been young when they'd separated, too unsure of himself and his future. He'd thought he'd failed when his marriage ended. He'd seen himself as a loser, believing he should have been able to solve his marriage issues. He should have been able to overcome adversity and make a go of it, as his own parents had.

Now he was a father and a businessman on a fast corporate track. He'd come through all these years relatively unscathed. He hadn't thought that possible when they'd first separated and subsequently divorced.

As he'd matured, he'd realized that being married to Lola was akin to trying to paint a room with only half the supplies. The effort was destined to fail.

The exact moment he'd realized this truth, he was able to cut his losses, realize the issues were beyond his control and move on. And so he'd closed the door on his youth and his ex-wife. He'd chalked that time of his life up to inexperience and naivety.

He couldn't be married without love, and what he and Lola had had was based on lust and duty. Neither element was a good foundation for any kind of permanence.

"Lola…" he began, then hesitated.

She gazed at him expectantly. Years ago, even after their separation, whenever she'd looked at him, he'd felt a flare of desire. He felt nothing now.

"Max?" she prompted, still waiting for him to continue.

"I'm glad you've changed, but that doesn't change anything between us," he said.

She seemed stunned by his statement. Her lower lip quivered. "What do you mean?"

He knew what she'd been fishing for, but he no longer wanted her that way. Praying she wouldn't start a tirade, he took a deep breath and began again, "We're still both Mandy's parents. That will never change. But we've been apart too long. I've become a different person. I don't want to rekindle anything with you. We got a great kid out of our marriage, which is more than some people have. I'll always be grateful to you for

Mandy. But I can't restart something I don't feel. I don't love you."

She looked as if he'd slapped her. "There's never been anyone but you for me."

"Lola, there have been many." To tell him otherwise was a bald-faced lie.

She shook her head. "Yes, but none that mattered. All those guys showed me was how great you and I had things and how stupid I was to have thrown that away. You care for me. You do."

Her hand trembled as her tone became anguished. "You've never dated anyone seriously. No one."

"That was because I wanted Mandy to have some stability in her life, not because I was pining for you. Mandy lives with me. You can date as many men as you want. I tried to counterbalance your actions by not dating. Perhaps that wasn't the best plan, but that's what I did."

"Oh, you're a candidate for sainthood," Lola snarled.

"Not trying for that, but I don't go for casual sex."

"Isn't that what your little bimbo is?" Lola asked, her voice cutting. "She's an actress, fitness trainer and goodness knows what else. I can't see her playing Suzy Homemaker and being Mrs. Harper."

"Maybe not, but I don't necessarily want to get married again. And I don't want to restart anything with you," Max said again, wondering why he was even bothering to explain. His ex would never understand. "Lola, it's best we keep our interactions cordial. We're Mandy's parents. But neither of us wants the other back."

"You used to," she reminded him, getting angrier by the second.

"Long ago, yes, I did. I won't even try to defend myself. But I'm no longer that person. I've changed."

She appeared ready to lose control. "Men always say that. It's just a pathetic excuse. It would be best for Mandy if we tried to work things out. She'd have both of her parents back together. We'd be a family. She's never really had that. She was a baby when we were together."

Max shook his head. "I don't think our reuniting and becoming a family would be wise, no matter the good intentions behind it. I don't love you anymore, Lola, and I never will again. Nothing you can do or say can change that. I don't want you. I want someone else." He paused, clarifying, "Or at least *something* else for my life."

"I hate you!" Lola shrieked and Max hoped she wouldn't throw anything. The autographed baseball sitting on his desk would make a pretty good missile. Lola's chest heaved and he knew she was reaching her boiling point.

"Perhaps you should go now," he suggested. "Calm down and think about what I said. You'll see I'm right. You don't want me. You're just in a funk since you're not in L.A. I'm sure you can get your career back on track."

"Even that little tramp has more acting credits than I have."

Max bristled. "Please don't speak that way about Terri."

Lola planted her hands on her hips. "I'll call her any name I want. She's a home wrecker. I'm not done with this, Max. I want my family back together and I'm not going to let anyone ruin it for me."

Max tried to pacify her. "Mandy's your family and she loves you a great deal. That will never change."

Lola began to pace. She whirled and faced him. "That's not what I mean. You're obviously not listening so I'll speak to you tomorrow. I'm too upset to continue this conversation tonight. Tell Mandy I love her and I'll call her."

Max moved to the living room and watched out his front window as Lola drove off in a huff. Mandy appeared then, taking her ear buds out. "Is Mom just leaving?"

"She and I had a few things to talk about," Max replied, glad his daughter hadn't overheard anything.

Mandy shrugged. "Oh. Okay. Anyway, I wanted to remind you that school registration is this week. Lynn's mom said she'll take me. And Lynn wants to know if I can spend the night tonight."

"That sounds fine. Hard to believe school's starting next week."

"It sucks," Mandy said.

"I'll want to see the clothes your mom bought for you."

"I figured. Don't worry. The dress code is being strictly enforced this year. I'm not being sent home to change. I bought school-appropriate stuff."

"Which is a smart idea because it would be Grandma coming to get you and me dealing with you later."

"Yeah, and Grandma scares me more than you do sometimes."

Max chuckled. His mother could be intense if the situation warranted. After all, she'd raised a bunch of boys.

"I'm going to go call Lynn. Her mom said she'd pick me up," Mandy finished.

"Be sure to say goodbye to me before you go."

"I will," Mandy said, heading back into her bedroom

to pack. Max returned to his office and sat at the desk. He sighed as he thought of Lola's tirade.

Why was it that when one thing went well, something else had to start going bad? Things with Terri were on a positive upswing, but this deal with Lola…

Max knew his ex far too well. Lola was nowhere near finished with this path she'd started treading. And since he'd just thwarted her first attempt at reconciliation, which he couldn't fathom why she wanted, anyway, he knew she'd be ticked off—and readying for round two.

CHAPTER TWELVE

"HEY MAX, I KNOW it's short notice, but do you think you could head to California this weekend?" Alan Henson stood in Max's doorway Wednesday afternoon.

"Yeah, sure. What's up?"

Alan had been scheduled to take the trip. Rocksolid was a major presence in the California insurance market and planned to host a suite at the track.

"My grandmother's dying and I'm going to have to fly to Portland, instead. We don't expect her to make it."

"I'm sorry," Max said immediately.

Alan gave a small smile. "Thanks. I appreciate it. She's ninety-eight and has lived a good, long life. She's not in any pain and she's told us she's ready to go meet Grandpa. I'm focusing on that."

Max nodded. "I'll clear my calendar."

"Perfect. I'll have Kathleen make your travel arrangements and put together your itinerary. If you need me, you have my cell number."

Max glanced at the clock when Alan left. He'd been meaning to call Terri. He'd sent her a flower arrangement on Monday as a thank-you for the weekend and she'd left him a voice mail saying she'd received them.

But Max hadn't had a moment since to call her back. He'd worked late, had meetings, and by the time he'd gotten home, he'd wanted to spend the last of his waking moments with Mandy.

He'd eased himself into bed around midnight, only to wake early and start over. Despite his exhaustion, he hadn't stopped thinking about Terri. Most women didn't interest him enough, and with time his most precious commodity, they easily got shuffled to the next day's to-do list, until after a week or so he'd lost interest totally.

Max groaned. He had another meeting in fifteen minutes. Not enough time, but better than nothing, since he hadn't spoken with her since Sunday. He reached for the phone and dialed.

When she answered, relief filled Max. He'd prayed he wouldn't get her voice mail yet again. "Hi," she said.

"Hi. I don't have long, but I didn't want you to think I was ignoring you. I've been suffering through meeting hell."

"I was wondering. Thank you again for the flowers. They're lovely."

"I'm glad you like them." He'd actually picked out the mixed-flower arrangement himself, instead of trusting it to his secretary. "Thanks for taking us. Mandy still can't stop talking about the trip."

"I remember my first time at the track. I think I bragged for days."

"I'd like to take you out again. This week is absolutely crazy, though, and my boss has to fly to Portland for a family emergency, meaning I'm doing double duty. What's the chance you'll be in California for the race?"

"I usually don't drive my motor home west of the Mississippi unless I'm taking a vacation. I try to stay within twelve hours of Charlotte. That's about my tolerance limit, since I do the driving myself."

"So you won't be there?" Disappointment consumed him.

"I really hadn't thought about it. I'm sure I could be. I can catch a ride on the PDQ jet."

"I'd love it if you came to California. I have to take Alan's place at the track this weekend. If you went, we could spend some time together. Alan always gets a suite, so if you'd like, you could stay in the extra bedroom."

"That could work," Terri replied.

"Then you'll go?"

"Let me think about it, check my schedule and call you tonight. Is that okay?" she asked.

"It's better than no," Max said, wishing she'd said yes outright. Of course, that was an unrealistic expectation, but he wanted to see her. If nothing else, not even speaking with her these past few days proved one thing—he didn't want to wait.

TERRI AGREED TO GO, and flew to California on the PDQ plane with her father.

"So you're going to meet the competition's sponsor again," Philip teased.

"Yep," Terri said.

Philip's expression turned serious. "But you like this man."

Terri nodded. "I do, and I don't know why. He's not like anyone else I've dated."

"Maybe that's why."

"Maybe," Terri said, her stomach becoming a bundle of nerves as the pilot announced their descent. She'd meet Bart in a hotel gym, but aside from that she had no obligations this weekend. The jet landed and Terri retrieved her luggage. PDQ had its team at another location, and they dropped her at Max's hotel.

When she retrieved her key from the front desk, the clerk handed her a note from Max telling her he had a meeting but would catch up with her in a few hours.

The suite was lovely. Two bedrooms flanked a large central living area big enough for entertaining. Her own bedroom came complete with fresh flowers and luxury linens. Despite all her travels, she'd never stayed anywhere so nice.

She'd settled in and was watching a movie when she heard the main door to the suite open. Max stepped inside.

She'd missed him. She watched as he set his briefcase on a table and began to loosen his tie. He wore a navy blue suit, and she swallowed the lump that formed in her throat. He looked divine. He had pure sex appeal and the character to go with it.

"Hi," she said, rising to her feet.

He gave her a wide smile. "Hey. You made it."

"I did."

"Good flight?"

"Smooth and easy," Terri said. She twisted her hands together as he stripped off the suit coat. Last weekend they'd been in her motor home. Even though the accommodations had been smaller, the space belonged to her, providing a sense of security. Now they were sharing a hotel suite and her nerves zinged.

"I know you love Italian food, but I was thinking of Mexican for dinner. There's an authentic place just one town over that three people recommended. I took the liberty of making a reservation."

"Sounds great," Terri said. He'd uncuffed his sleeves. This must be what he looked like every day when he came home. She'd dressed casually in capris and a sweater, so she guessed he'd want to change before dinner.

"Do you mind if I clean up?" he asked, confirming her suspicions.

"No. Take your time."

Within an hour they were at the restaurant, sitting in a booth drinking the establishment's signature margaritas.

Terri rolled the flavor over her tongue. "This is good."

"Sorry I was a bit distant when I walked in the door," Max replied. He reached out and held her hand. "I'm usually somewhat frazzled after a long day at work. I thought about how rude I was while in the shower. Not a good first impression at all."

"It's not like we're used to each other."

"No, we aren't. I apologize. I guess that's what made it so awkward."

"But understandable. When my dad gets home, he needs a half hour of downtime before dinner." She paused. "So how did things go today?"

"It was an intense but rewarding day. I'm doing all Alan's jobs, and he's a top executive, so filling his shoes is a real learning experience."

"I'm sure you're up to the challenge."

He seemed excited. "I am. It's what I've been working for my whole life."

She smiled in complete understanding.

AFTER DINNER, she and Max went back to the hotel, forgoing the suite for the hotel's intimate dance club. The venue catered to an older crowd, the music tending more toward swing and ballroom than modern, and Terri found Max an excellent instructor as he taught her some moves that didn't involve hip-hop steps.

They also involved holding her close, and Terri found her cheek pressed to his chest. As he gathered her tightly in his arms, the heat between them began to build.

He'd hugged her before and kissed her, but dancing suggested the intimacy of lovemaking. They swayed together, their legs intertwined, bodies with no space between. Her senses were on overdrive; music filled her ears, and her fingers curled into his shirt, feeling the hardness of the muscles beneath. Every breath brought her the scent so uniquely him, and her eyes closed as she savored the moment.

But then the music increased in tempo, and Terri realized she didn't want the contact to end. "Time to go," he whispered, as if reading her mind.

She nodded and they returned to the suite. The maid had left on only one lamp, which cast the living room in a low glow. The safety of soft darkness was what she needed now, as Max once again lowered his mouth to hers.

Terri kissed him back, allowing herself to be wrapped

in the velvety cocoon of his arms, his deep soothing voice occasionally whispering in her ear.

"Take me to your room," she said.

Max leaned back. "Are you sure? It might change everything."

"It's okay."

"I don't think I'll ever get my fill of you, but before we start this, I have to tell you, my work and daughter come first."

She appreciated his honesty. "I can live with that. Mine does, too."

"I can't promise forever," he warned again. "And Lola—"

"She's not here. And you and I are not talking about forever. We've promised each other to take each day as it comes."

"If you're sure."

"Never more so," Terri said, and with that, she let him lead the way.

A WEEK LATER, by the time Terri parked her motor home in the infield Drivers' and Owners' lot at Richmond, she was a lot more comfortable and confident in her relationship with her two passengers. Not only had she and Max spent the entire weekend in California together, but they had managed to see each other once they'd returned.

While neither had promised to make the other a priority, making love had been like opening a dam. They couldn't get enough of each other, and had tried to see each other as much as possible, even if it was only an hour over lunch. They started talking on the phone late at night, as well, sometimes until two in the morning.

"You're getting to see a lot of the country this way," Max told Mandy as they exited the motor home.

"I don't mind. I'm just excited Jill's here." Jill was one of the drivers' daughters whom Mandy had met at summer camp. So tonight Terri and Max would watch the NASCAR Nationwide Series race from a suite and Mandy would sleep over in her new friend's family's motor home.

"So, back again?" Bart teased Max when he saw him later that night. They were watching the NASCAR Nationwide Series and everyone in his sponsor's suite was cheering for PDQ's team.

"Couldn't stay away," Max said as he shook Bart's hand. "Thanks for getting Terri and me in here with you."

"Ah, anything for Terri. You've been distracting her and for that I'm grateful."

Max arched an eyebrow. "Really?"

Bart laughed. "Oh, yeah, when she's happy, she doesn't make me work as hard. Don't let her train you. She can be a real slave driver."

Terri, who'd been listening to the conversation, punched Bart lightly in the arm. "Don't you say that. I'm going to make you run an extra two miles on Monday just because."

"Ow." Bart rubbed his arm even though she hadn't hit him hard. "See what I mean? She's a brute. Keep distracting her for me, okay?"

"I'll try," Max promised, sending Terri a look that indicated he planned to do exactly that later tonight.

She blushed a little. Everyone at the track knew they were an item, and several had told her they'd never seen her happier.

Terri had to admit they were right. The beginning of a relationship was often wonderful, but in many cases, the bloom fell off the rose quickly. However, she and Max had grown much closer over the past week.

Their desire for each other showed no sign of ebbing, but at the same time they were developing a closeness that went beyond the physical. They had a mental and emotional connection.

Max touched her elbow, and Terri realized she hadn't been listening to Bart.

Terri covered the inattention by changing the subject. "So are you going to win tomorrow night?"

"I've hit the top ten the last two races," Bart said.

"Tell you what. You get in the Chase by the end of this race, and I'll let you have Monday off. There's your incentive."

He eyed her suspiciously. "You mean I won't have to work out?"

She clarified. "Yes. You just need a top-twelve finish."

"I'm going to win so I can have a day off. That's the best incentive I've had. Well, that and I said if I won I'd donate the trophy to the local children's hospital."

A collective groan came from the group as the caution flag came out. The PDQ car had gotten caught in a wreck. While the driver hadn't caused the accident, his car needed some work. He'd lose a lot of track position as his crew worked on the repairs.

"I hope this doesn't happen tomorrow night," Bart

said as the TV announcer relayed they'd reached a record number of race cautions.

"It'll be fine," Terri reassured Bart. "Just get your car and my dad into victory lane."

"Planning on it," Bart said.

"So do you think he'll win?" Max asked once Bart moved out of earshot.

Terri nodded. "I think he can. He's got a lot of raw talent. I wish I'd had all that."

"No remorse," Max reminded her. "Just think, I wouldn't have met you if you'd still been racing."

"True," Terri acknowledged. She slid her arm through his. Since the race was almost over, she'd lost interest. She had other, more important things on her mind. "What do you say we beat the traffic and watch the rest of this from the TV in my motor home?"

"You mean that plasma screen in your bedroom?"

"That'd be the one," Terri said.

Max dropped a light kiss on her lips. "I think that's the best idea I've heard all night."

THE NEXT DAY Max, Mandy and Terri watched the NASCAR Sprint Cup Series race from the top of Bart's hauler. Sometimes Terri would watch from Bart's pit box, and other times from a suite if one of Bart's sponsors hosted. However, this time there hadn't been room for three more people in the suite, and because Max also had loyalty to the Billy Budd camp, they'd decided that seeing the race from a hauler roof would be just fine.

They had a perfect view of the entire track, and she'd

brought up a portable television so they could follow what was going on.

"You can tell everyone's trying to make the Chase," Terri said as the race entered its final sixty laps. The drivers would complete a total of four hundred laps tonight, which was three hundred miles.

Six guys existed on the bubble, including Bart and Will. If the Branch twins didn't place inside the top fifteen by tonight's checkered flag, they risked being outside the top twelve in driver points. That meant they wouldn't be contenders in the Chase for the NASCAR Sprint Cup Series, which began the next weekend in New Hampshire.

About four drivers raced, not for the top twelve, but for owner's points. Those drivers simply wanted to get their respective owners in the top thirty-five, guaranteeing their cars spots in Daytona the following February. At each race some drivers had to race their way in based on qualifying position, and if they didn't make the field of forty-three, then their teams loaded up the haulers and everyone went home to watch the race on TV.

The words "There's always next weekend" ceased being true tonight. After Richmond only twelve drivers would contend for the NASCAR Sprint Cup Series championship with points reset. The previous season Kent Grosso hadn't been the points leader starting the Chase for the NASCAR Sprint Cup, but he'd driven well and racked up wins, dropping the points leader to second by Homestead and thus claiming the trophy for himself. In racing, nothing was ever set in stone.

So, as the night continued, Terri broke down and succumbed to her nervous habit of gnawing on her fingernails. Bart and Will had skated through the four cautions. Five cars had retired from the race after being damaged so badly they couldn't continue.

A light breeze blew, making the warm night palatable. Bugs swarmed the track lights, adding a frantic feel. The lead had changed six times, with Kent Grosso currently gracing the top of the scoring pylon.

However, everyone had to pit. Not one driver could finish without taking fuel. As they'd finally hit a stretch of good green-flag racing, no one wanted to be caught on pit road, have a caution flag fly and then be stuck a lap down. A leader could find himself a loser if that happened, making pit strategy pivotal.

Terri used her binoculars and scanned the area where the spotters stood. She could tell the teams were cutting deals and negotiating with one another about when to pit. The television commentators confirmed what she'd observed, saying they'd overheard a conversation between current champ Dean Grosso and his crew chief telling him to pit on Lap 360.

That meant the leaders should all come down at once with a few drivers at the back of the pack staying out.

"Here they come," Mandy shouted as Kent Grosso hit the brakes and entered pit road. He had a stall halfway down and after he pulled in, the television showed a closeup. If Kent could get out in thirteen seconds or less, he'd be doing great.

Pit road was crowded. Pole winner Rafael O'Bryan had chosen the first pit stall. He'd have an easy exit, but getting down to the end of pit road from his current position of fifteen was proving tricky. The race off pit road could be desperate. A driver blocked Dean Grosso in. Dean had to back up to get out, almost clipping the front tire changer of the team behind him.

Terri winced for the crew member as he jumped out of way, the incident costing valuable time for both teams.

"How'd Bart do?" Max asked. He craned his neck, watching pit road. Bart had been in twentieth position before his pit stop.

"He picked up five places," Mandy announced, her gaze glued to the television. "Will's moved up to tenth."

"You know, if those brothers worked together they might get somewhere," Max said.

"Even though they aren't teammates, I have a feeling they'll do just that," Terri replied. At least she hoped so. Quite a few brothers raced at the NASCAR Sprint Cup Series level. Sometimes the guys had their differences, but for the most part, family was family. They could race against each other in the final laps.

The caution flag flew ten laps later as a rookie driver got loose, overcorrected and crashed into the Turn Two wall. Not one driver who'd pitted under the green flag came down pit road once it opened. The leaders all stayed out. They had enough fuel to make it to the end of the race, which was now all about track position.

As a few other drivers fell back, Bart and Will had both moved into the top ten.

"Top ten if they can hold it," Terri said. She was already chewing on her nails, but she hadn't yet bit them. If she didn't watch herself, she'd start, she was that nervous. She wanted this for Bart, but mostly she wanted a win for her father. He'd worked so hard on getting the car ready.

Bart created a hole by going three wide in the backstretch. He snuck by two lap-down cars and then, with Will on his bumper, passed both Hart Hampton and Rafael O'Bryan.

"He's now seventh!" Mandy yelled. Bart had truly become *her* driver, the one she cheered for over everyone else.

"He's still going," Max said.

"I'm just as surprised as you are!" Terri shouted. She jumped to her feet, unable to sit still. Bart and his brother were on fire. They were racing clean, but they were racing hard. They had five laps to go and the cars were averaging speeds of a hundred miles an hour, give or take a little, meaning their lap times around the short track were somewhere around twenty-nine seconds.

With four laps to go, the tag team of Bart and Will Branch had reached the top three. Kent Grosso had dropped out of the top ten; currently he fought to keep his eleventh spot.

With three laps left, Bart's No. 475 picked off the third-place car of Dean Grosso, sending him behind to battle Will's No. 407.

Will, not to be left behind, passed Dean high on Turn Two. Only Justin Murphy's car, No. 448, stood in Bart's way of making a trip to victory lane. Bart also had to battle his brother, who, now that they were at the end, wasn't about to let Bart simply coast across the finish line in front.

However, Bart hadn't been in victory lane since Charlotte in May, and he was hungry for a win. Terri stood on the edge of the hauler, Mandy and Max at her side. Tension filled the air—even the bugs seemed to flitter faster in their dance beneath the lights.

Bart, Justin and Will went three wide in the backstretch. The engines roared as they accelerated on the straightaway between Turn Two and Turn Three.

Terri's eyes widened. "Oh, my. I don't believe it! Justin's falling back!"

As if realizing the Branch brothers were on something akin to a suicide mission, Justin had given up the game of chicken and dropped safely into third as he entered Turn Three. Bart and Will were nose on nose in the battle for first and second place. Bart had the high line, while Will hugged the inside groove. Bart shot off Turn Four, and as they came down the front stretch to the start-finish line, the race was literally too close to call. Terri ran to the television. The cameras all around the track would see the fraction of a second separating the cars better than she could.

The two brothers flew like bats out of hell, with one car barely nosing out the other…

"He did it!" Terri didn't realize she was sobbing as Bart edged past Will and took the checkered flag. "He won!"

The television showed her dad in the pit box, getting hugs from his team.

"Whoo-hoo!" Mandy threw both hands into the air and gave her dad a high five before giving Terri one. Terri didn't realize that she'd been trembling until Mandy's palm connected with hers.

"You okay?" Max asked, concerned.

"Fine. Happy. Come on, we need to get to victory lane." Terri was jubilant.

"We're going to victory lane?" Mandy asked.

"Yes," Terri said, the enormity of the win hitting her like a lightning bolt. Bart had snapped his winless streak. He'd raced clean and hard. He'd made the Chase!

"Hey, Terri! You coming?" One of the team members stood below the ladder of the hauler. He'd raced back for something.

"We'll be right there," Terri yelled.

Max reached over and gave her a hug and a kiss. "Come on. Let's go celebrate, shall we?"

Terri dried her eyes on her sleeve. "Let's."

VICTORY LANE could best be described as controlled chaos. Those in the media had their positions clearly marked and stood on risers surrounding the area. Team members waited behind the car, up against the backdrop.

PDQ owner Jim Latimer was there with his team, his smile wide, thrilled his driver had brought home a win. Philip Whalen's eyes had a sheen that Terri recognized as happy tears, but if asked, her dad would claim the moisture was from dust or champagne spray.

On the given signal, Bart climbed out, stood on the door and raised his arms above his head. His team immediately doused him from head to toe with champagne and he yelled in jubilation before jumping down. His first hugs came from Philip and Jim, and then the television reporter shoved the microphone in his face and asked him how winning felt.

"The best, man," Bart answered, wiping off his face with the towel Anita Wolcott handed him. "Racing my brother and beating him is always the best. It makes this win really special. We haven't raced like that in a while."

"Speaking of…" the reporter said as Will Branch entered victory lane and jumped on his brother in a show of congratulations.

"That was some kickin' racing," Will said. He smiled for the cameras, the two brothers so identical, framed perfectly. "Next time, though, you're going down!"

Bart laughed at his brother's assertion and then answered a few more questions as Will left the area. They'd meet up in the media center later. Then, seeing Terri and Mandy, Bart gestured them over.

"No workout for me!" Bart shouted, encircling Terri in his arms and planting a big kiss on her lips. "Don't you forget that!"

"Don't you forget that workouts helped get you here!" Terri laughed as he released her. "I'm proud of you! You're in the Chase!"

"And it's great! Hey, there's my number-one fan!" Bart lifted Mandy and spun her around. Then he took off his ball cap and stuck the hat on Mandy's head. From her expression, Mandy didn't care that it was soaked with champagne.

Then Anita was there to manage things, working in the capacity of both fiancée of the team owner and Bart's PR rep.

Since the race was on Saturday night, Terri and Max had decided to make a stop in colonial Williamsburg so they could see some historic sites on the way home. The trip back to Charlotte was only four hours, so they had time.

They returned to the hauler, cleaned off the roof and returned the lawn chairs and television to their proper storage places. Then they began the trek to the motor home lot, careful to avoid teams moving everything from cars to war wagons.

"So why did Bart kiss you?" Mandy asked as they showed their credentials at the security gate. Most of the drivers and their families had rented cars and were on their way to the airport, their motor-home drivers taking charge of getting their homes-away-from-home back to Charlotte. Mandy had already said goodbye to her friend Jill.

"Bart kissed me just because," Terri said, highly aware of Max walking at her side. He'd tensed a little on hearing his daughter's question.

"People do that?" Mandy asked.

"Bart's like my brother, and he was excited because I told him if he won I wouldn't make him work out. So in a sense he was celebrating."

"Adults are weird," Mandy stated.

That cut the seriousness of the situation and, unable to help himself, Max laughed and ruffled her hair. "Dad! I told you not to do that!" Mandy protested.

"That's what you get for saying I'm weird," Max teased.

"Well, that just proves you are." Mandy ducked out of reach as he tried again. They'd reached the motor home and Mandy opened the door. She paused on the step. "You two coming?"

"In a minute," Max said. "I want to talk to Terri a moment first."

"Okay, but no kissing. People might see you. It's embarrassing."

"Embarrassing to do this?" Terri said, leaning over and giving Max a quick kiss.

"Ugh!" Mandy said, and she disappeared out of sight, the door closing behind her. Both Terri and Max were laughing.

"So what did you want to talk about?" Terri asked.

"BART KISSED YOU," Max said simply.

"We're just friends," Terri replied, and Max could see the worry in her eyes.

"I know."

"Then I don't understand."

He'd obviously confused her. He leaned against the motor home. "I don't entirely, either. Back when I was dating Lola, she loved to flirt with other guys. I got jealous. I'd have these urges to say something."

"You have no reason to be jealous about me," she said.

"That's not what I felt," Max said.

Her eyes widened. "No?"

He was still trying to sort it out himself. "No. I felt…trust. In you. Understanding and acceptance that it was just a kiss between friends."

Terri nodded.

"So unlike with Lola," he went on, "I had a sense that you wouldn't do anything to jeopardize us." He jerked a hand through his hair. The black locks were a bit sticky with champagne—everyone in Bart's general vicinity had gotten sprayed.

Terri reached out and touched his arm, and he grabbed her hand, her touch a comfort to him.

"I'm not saying I *like* other guys kissing you, but I knew it was innocent. I guess I should explain more. Aside from her flirting, Lola used to really get into her local theater roles. If the characters had to kiss…well, I don't think Lola needed to practice as hard as she did. I think she just enjoyed making me squirm."

"I would never do that," Terri said. She placed her free hand on top of their conjoined ones and he relaxed a little.

"It was an odd way to get a revelation. I knew that the kiss was totally innocent without you having to tell me. I never had that connection with Lola."

"She did a number on you, didn't she?" Terri said. She freed her hand and reached up to stroke Max's jaw. She let herself feel the rough stubble of his five-o'clock shadow, and Max let himself memorize the texture of her fingers. Then she reached up to cup his face before bringing his mouth down to hers for a kiss.

Her mouth worked its magic, almost as if a kiss could erase the pain of the past. With Terri he felt hope and purity, as if life could actually be all good.

"This is getting very serious," Max told Terri when they stopped kissing a few minutes later. "I think I'm falling for you."

"I know," Terri replied. His heart froze for a moment until she said, "But I'm falling for you, too. That makes two of us on this slippery slope."

"I'll hold on if you do," he said, giving her a lopsided grin.

She smiled and touched his face again. He captured her hand and kissed her palm.

"Hey, Terri, get a room. What's the use of that big old bus if you don't use it?" one of the older, grizzled motorhome drivers shouted as he went by.

"I guess we should take this inside," Max said.

"Mandy," Terri reminded him.

"Okay, postponed until later, although I was referring to our conversation. Your mind was in the gutter."

She playfully punched him. "You are so funny. See if you get any at all."

"I bet I can tempt you."

"Yeah, probably. I'm such a pushover where you're concerned." Terri laughed as she brushed by him and entered the code to open the door.

As he walked up the steps, Max realized exactly how much he cared for Terri. Unlike Lola, who'd annoyed him pretty quickly once they'd gotten married, Max had a sudden vision of being with Terri when they were old and gray.

They simply understood each other on all the levels that mattered and in all the ways needed to make a relationship work. The thought petrified him. He'd never thought he'd get married again, had made it a point of pride that he wasn't a guy desperate for a wife. Was he changing his mind?

"You coming?" Terri asked.

Max dismissed his fear and stepped inside. "You know I'd follow you anywhere."

Terri's eyes darkened a little as she caught his double meaning. "Good." She stroked his cheek one last time, indicating she felt the same way. "Then let's get out of here."

CHAPTER THIRTEEN

TERRI WAS at her studio Tuesday when the front bell tinkled, indicating someone had arrived. Because the studio was located in the interior of a small office building and had no storefront window, she never had drop-ins.

Terri frowned at the intrusion. The mail always arrived by ten. Her next client wasn't due until three and it was only one-thirty. She'd spent most of the afternoon so far catching up on paperwork and organizing her schedule. The first race of the Chase for the NASCAR Sprint Cup would be at New Hampshire, Dover would be the race location after that. She planned on being at both.

Rounding out September would be Kansas, but Terri wouldn't drive her motor home there, for that drive was almost fifteen hours. Bart, who'd credited her for his improved physique, could manage one race without her. He could always use the fitness facility in the hotel the team stayed at. She'd design a routine for him to follow.

As promised she'd given Bart the day off yesterday, his reward for doing well and making her dad happy. Bart's win had marked Philip's sixtieth overall win as a crew chief. Terri rose and left her office, heading out into the main fitness area.

Max's ex-wife, Lola, was waiting for her.

"Interesting how these things can make men so much better-looking," Lola said, running her fingers along one of the chrome weight bars.

Terri had never seen Lola dressed down, and today was no exception. Lola wore a pair of strappy high heels, designer capris, a tight sweater and a scarf at her waist to tie it all together. Her sunglasses were poking from the top of a purse that Terri knew had cost hundreds.

"Is there something I can help you with?" Terri asked, willing herself to keep her hands from clenching into fists at her sides. This was her territory. Lola was the interloper.

"Out in L.A. all the stars have personal trainers," Lola said, sashaying closer to Terri. "I had one for a little while, too. You can have a trainer for just about anything—your body, your voice, even your acting ability. Have you ever seen some stars' entourages? They can easily have twenty people. Rappers have even more."

"I'm not into rap," Terri said, wishing Lola would get to the point of her visit. She clearly had an agenda.

"I don't like rap, either, but rappers do throw the best parties," Lola confided. She glanced around. "So this is your studio. Has Max seen it?"

"He's been here," Terri replied. She chose not to tell Lola she'd missed her ex by about an hour. Max had stopped by for lunch.

"Mandy said she had a good time at Richmond. Although I don't know why she won't let anyone wash that sticky old hat."

"Because it's Bart Branch's from victory lane," Terri

said. "He took it straight off his head and gave it to her."
Any race fan would understand the significance.

Lola exhaled a dramatic sigh designed to convey
without words how silly she thought that was.

"I'm assuming you're not here over a hat." Terri
crossed her arms.

"No, of course not. It's at Max's, anyway," Lola said,
wrinkling her nose. "He's the reason I'm here. I figured
it was probably time you and I talked."

"Okay." Terri gestured to a chair, but no one sat.

"I *am* Mandy's mother," Lola stated, and Terri heard
the steel in the other woman's voice. "That's a very important fact everyone seems to be forgetting lately. You
see, I would appreciate it if you backed off. You aren't
her mother. You aren't even her stepmother. You're just
some woman Max happens to fancy at the moment.
He's never lasted very long with anyone and I really
would prefer it if Mandy didn't grow any more attached
to you. It'll just make things rough when Max gets tired
of you and moves on."

Terri's fingers dug into her arms as she attempted to
absorb everything Lola had let loose. "I don't think he's
going to get tired of me," Terri said.

Lola blinked, her expression sympathetic. "Well, then
I feel sorry for you. If you're smart, you'll wise up and
tire of him first. He's not going to marry you. Hasn't he
made that clear? Max is as anti-marriage as they come."

"We're not talking marriage." Terri held her ground,
refusing to let Lola know she'd hit a nerve. She and Max
had once said that neither wanted to get married. But
now…well, where would things end up if they stayed

together? They'd grown closer. People who ended up happily in love got married, didn't they? It was a conversation for another time, and Terri had been comfortable with that—until now.

Lola's black eyes narrowed. "I didn't leave Max because of his bad habits. I loved my husband. We were just too young. If we'd had more time before Mandy came along, I'm sure things would have been different."

"Maybe," Terri said.

"Not that I ever regretted my daughter's arrival," Lola added. "But children really do change a relationship. They put a strain on it. You're always tired because you're up all night. You can't make love for eight weeks after a C-section."

Lola shifted her weight. "You don't make love much before the birth, and after you're cleared for sex, you still have all this unsightly weight to lose. Those things can take a toll on a relationship, especially when you're as young as we were. Our sex life finally came back after our divorce."

Terri frowned and Lola smiled slightly. "Oh, I see he hasn't told you about those times. Max has never been able to resist me. Even after our divorce. Now I recognize those times for what they were. He'll always want me and what we had."

"I assure you, I'm keeping him quite busy and very happy," Terri said. This whole conversation was making her uncomfortable. "As for Mandy, she's twelve. She's an intelligent girl. I'm sure she's adjusting just fine to the new circumstances. She told me Sunday that she's thrilled her dad's dating me."

"I want you to stay away from Max and Mandy," Lola blurted out, her face reddening slightly.

"That's not going to happen," Terri said, well aware Lola's control was slipping fast now that she wasn't getting her way.

Lola drew herself up. "It needs to happen," she stressed, her warning clear. "I came back to Charlotte with the intention of putting my family back together. You are ruining it for everyone. If you care about Max and Mandy, you'll do what's best for them and break this silliness off now."

"No." The word left Terri's mouth like a bullet and hung out in the air defiantly. Lola's mouth dropped open slightly. Had the woman never had anyone cross her?

"You'd destroy their lives?" Lola shot back.

Terri shook her head. She wanted a relationship with Max and she'd fight for it. She wasn't one to back down and she had to trust that Max cared for her. "I'm not the one ruining things. *You* are."

"Hardly!" Lola snapped.

"You're deluding yourself if you believe Max wants to get back together with you. He and I care about each other and you aren't a part of our future. Well, except as Mandy's mother. You will always have that connection to him. But that's it. I'm not going to stop seeing someone I care about because of your misguided notions."

"How dare you!" Lola's anger was intensifying.

Terri silently counted to ten. "Lola, I'm not wasting any more of my valuable time on this inane conversation. I'm not breaking up with Max just because you've decided you want him back. Life doesn't work that way.

You need to do what he did and move on. It's probably beyond time."

"I'm just going to leave you with the following warning," Lola said coldly. "I always get what I want."

Terri couldn't help herself. "Oh, please," she said. "If that were true, you'd have an Oscar."

"I'll show you," Lola said. Then she spun on her heel and strode to the door and out.

Terri exhaled the breath she'd been holding. She wore her yoga clothes, and she immediately moved into "mountain pose" as she tried to calm her mind and return her heartbeat to normal.

Lola had upset Terri far more than Terri had let on. She suddenly needed to hear Max's voice. She picked up her office phone and dialed the number she'd committed to memory. Her fingers clutched the receiver as the ringing started. *Please, not voice mail.*

"Max Harper."

"Oh, you're there." Relief washed over her.

He must have heard her stress. "Terri, are you okay?"

"I am, now that I'm talking to you," she said. "Tell me that you care for me."

"I didn't show you enough earlier today?" He chuckled and then sobered as he realized something wasn't right. "What happened?"

"Lola stopped by the studio." The calm she'd achieved from the yoga pose fled when she said those words.

"And?" he prompted.

"She wants me to back off. She wants to put her family back together. She told me she's planning on taking you away from me."

Terri felt a panic unlike any she'd ever experienced, even that time she'd crashed her truck into the wall at Talladega at 170 miles an hour. "If you're going back to her, please tell me now."

"I don't love her," Max said. "Let me clear my afternoon and I'll be right over. I think you need a hug and I'm just the guy to give it to you. Did you hear me? I'm your guy."

A tear slid down Terri's face. "Thank you."

"I'll be there in about twenty minutes."

Reassured now, she remembered her schedule. "No, you don't have to do that. You're working and I have a client coming. But will you see me afterward? Tonight?"

"You don't even have to ask. Just name the time. I'll have my mother keep Mandy for the evening. She'll already be there since she goes to my mom's after school."

"My client leaves at four. I'll be at your house by five at the latest."

"And I'll be there waiting for you," Max promised.

"Thank you," Terri whispered.

MAX SPOKE with Terri for a couple of more minutes before he set the phone down. He glanced at his schedule. When September had arrived, he'd been moved to another Rocksolid division. This division involved a lot more meetings and report writing, but his afternoon was mercifully clear. He picked up his phone and let his secretary know he'd be leaving at three and to inform anyone who might come by or call. He wanted to get home and make sure everything was perfect before Terri arrived.

He next phoned Brice. While he didn't technically have to get his boss's approval to skip out early, a lot was riding on the Rising Stars Program and he didn't want to make a misstep. Clearing things with Brice was a formality.

"So you're covered?" Brice asked after Max let him know he was leaving.

"My secretary knows to call me at home if there's an emergency I must handle," Max said.

"There won't be and if there is, don't worry about it. I'll deal with whatever comes up."

"Thanks," Max replied.

"Do you mind if I ask what it is?" Brice asked. Max knew he could trust him.

"My ex-wife stopped by my girlfriend's and told her she wants me back. Needless to say, Terri's a little upset."

"So you and Terri are serious?" Brice said.

"I hope so." Max still had fears, but he was becoming less afraid each day.

"Well, out of the two, Terri's got my vote. You've been more productive and much happier lately. She's good for you. I like her already and I've never even met her. Everyone's noticed a real positive change in you."

"I didn't realize I was that miserable before," Max said.

Brice's rich laugh traveled over the line. "Not miserable, just not...alive. Heck, I love my job, but I don't let it consume me like you do."

"I'm just trying to make a better future for my family."

"And no one faults you for that. As I said before, you've impressed everyone upstairs, and that's saying something. Now go get your private life sorted out. Rocksolid will survive for a few hours without you."

"Thanks," Max said. He hung up the phone and looked around. He loved his job, but since meeting Terri his priorities had changed slightly. Terri had moved up into the top slots defining his life. No way was he going to let Lola scare her off.

LOLA LAID LOW until the day before Max flew to New Hampshire. After Max had reassured Terri Tuesday night how he felt about her, he hadn't been naive enough to think his ex-wife wouldn't make some sort of dramatic statement. But Wednesday and Thursday had passed without a peep. Lola waited until Friday afternoon, when she'd picked Mandy up for her weekend visit, before ripping into him.

Oh, she'd tried to be sweet and sexy first, but when he'd rejected her ensuing advances, she'd turned mean. The argument with Lola had shaken him to the core, but he hadn't wanted to ruin his weekend with Terri by bringing the subject up.

This was their first weekend since California where it was only the two of them at the race track. The weather in New Hampshire didn't yet reflect the autumnal equinox, although the official date of that was still a week away. For all intents and purposes, summer was still clinging to the East Coast, refusing to let fall occur without a fight.

There was also a championship battle gearing up and readying to start in a few hours in the NASCAR Craftsman Truck Series. Two drivers were separated by only twenty points. They'd been trading the top two spots back and forth for months, and neither was yet the clear series victor.

Max had missed NASCAR Sprint Cup Series qualifying, which had actually occurred Friday afternoon
before the NASCAR Camping World Series East race
Friday night. The NASCAR Craftsman Truck Series
dominated the track Saturday, with a NASCAR Whelen
Modified Tour race occurring between NASCAR
Craftsman Truck Series qualifying and the actual race.

He'd flown directly into the infield with Jim Latimer,
a real eye-opening experience, as it had been Max's
first helicopter ride. It was Jim's chosen method of
transportation once the PDQ plane landed at the New
Hampshire airport. Max had no idea how Terri had
arranged all this for him, but Jim had been a great com-
panion, and in addition to making small talk, they'd
also discussed Rocksolid's sponsorship of Billy Budd.

Max had sensed that Jim was perhaps feeling him out
about the opportunity to change forces and sponsor Bart
somewhere in the future, but Max didn't want to be pre-
sumptuous. In fact, all he cared about at this moment
was that it was late Saturday afternoon and he wanted
to find Terri.

He found her by Bart's hauler, talking with her dad.
"Hey," he said.

Her eyes seemed to light up the moment she saw him.
A powerful feeling swept over him. He couldn't quite
describe it, but he reveled in the hug she gave him and
her simple "Hi."

"Everything going well?" he asked, itching to touch
her beyond the hug they'd shared. The infield was a
flurry of activity, but Max's attention narrowed to the
woman in front of him. She was all he wanted.

"We hope so," she replied.

"Good." His focus was not on Bart's chances but rather his own. She completed him, and he needed her.

"Are you free?"

She smiled and took his hand. "I've just been waiting for you."

They ended up missing almost the entire NASCAR Craftsman Truck race, catching the end on television once they finally left the bedroom of Terri's motor home in search of a late dinner. Max hadn't meant to make love all afternoon, but today's lovemaking had had a sense of urgency, a desire for something deeper than simple physical release. They wanted that connection that two people who care deeply for each other share.

Now that their stomachs were full and they were satiated, he tickled the arch of Terri's bare left foot as they sat next to each other on the sofa. She squeaked and drew her feet underneath her. "Stop that."

"What?" He reached over and tickled her on the waist. "You mean this?"

"Yes," she said, squirming to get away from him. "You're evil. I need my rest."

"No. No rest for the weary," he teased. Then, on a serious note, he reached for her and drew her safely into the crook of his arm and they watched the last few laps. The race leader had a commanding lead and no one could catch him, so the finish was nowhere near as exciting as Bart and Will's shootout the weekend before.

Max ran his fingers through her reddish-brown hair, savoring the silken texture. "I don't think I'll ever get enough of you," he told her. "You know how I feel."

"Do I?" she asked.

"I hope you've realized I love you." The words hung out there and he leaned closer so he could look into her eyes. The outer rim was darker than the center, and perhaps that was why her gaze always drew him in. It was important for her to know how deep his feelings ran.

She snuggled closer for a minute, as if listening to his heartbeat.

Then she drew back a little so she could see his face. "Something's wrong, isn't it? Is it that I didn't say the words back to you?"

"No." He gave her a reassuring smile. He didn't want to push her into a declaration she didn't feel. "I'm just really happy being here with you."

"You should know I love you," Terri said.

"You don't have to tell me that just because I said it."

"I know," Terri said. "But I do love you. I mean it." He heard the conviction in her voice. "And I *like* you a lot. I like the way we fit and how we relate. You're here in my world. You haven't asked me to stay home and hang out in the kitchen. You don't want me to stop working or give up my lifestyle. I appreciate that. Even though I haven't seen them lately, my friends Pam and Libby are dying to meet you."

"I don't want to take up all your leisure time," Max insisted. As much as he loved her, it was true. Monopolizing Terri's time would be unhealthy for both of them.

She smiled reassuringly. "You're much more fun than they are. And I certainly don't want to sleep with either of them."

He laughed. "That's good to know."

"Isn't it? See how lucky you are?" Terri snuggled against him and he pulled her close. He loved holding her. "So tell," she said. "What's really going on? I know there's something besides your declaration. I can sense it."

He sighed. If he loved Terri, he'd share everything with her. "Lola's not backing down."

"Did she finally throw her hissy fit?"

"It was a little more than that," Max admitted. He watched as Terri eased herself up so she could look at him.

"Don't tell me she threw herself at you."

He shook his head. "Not exactly. Well, not after I told her nothing was going to happen between us."

"She didn't take it very well?"

"Not really. I'm worried about Mandy being with her all weekend, too. Who *knows* what she'll say. Do you mind if I check on Mandy? I should see if she called."

"No, of course not. If she called, call her back. She'll want to talk to you. Tell her I said hi."

Max checked his voice mail and frowned. His daughter had left two messages. He pressed speed dial. It was still early enough for Mandy to be awake.

She answered her cell on the second ring. "Hi, Dad."

"Hey, sorry I didn't have my phone on. What's up?"

"I'm bored," Mandy said, and Max's heart gave a little lurch. "I watched the truck race. Did you see it?"

"Just the end. So where's your mom?"

"I don't know. I'm here by myself. Mom's out. She got a phone call and told me she had to go out. Then she left."

Great parenting, Max thought, trying to contain his anger, especially after the conversation he and Lola just had. "I'm sure she had something important to do," he said.

"She told me not to wait up. If I'm just going to sit here, I'd rather be there. I'm sure you and Terri are having a much better time."

"We wish you were here, too. It was your mother's weekend and she demanded that you go with her."

"Yeah, only to leave me by myself. Lynn's at another friend's or I'd call her and go over there."

"Why don't you call your grandma Harper and have her come pick you up? In fact, let me call her and I'll call you back."

"Nah. Mom'll just get mad. I just heard the car door. I'll talk to you tomorrow."

"I'm sorry I didn't see this coming. I love you."

"Me, too," Mandy said.

Max ended the call and set his phone down. He saw Terri's concerned expression. "Lola took off and left Mandy by herself. She has no idea where Lola went. But it looks like she's home now."

"She's only twelve," Terri protested.

"Almost thirteen. Her birthday's at the end of the month. She's old enough to babysit, but she's still too young to be left at home by herself at night. I'll be discussing this with Lola, that's for sure."

"That's irresponsible."

"I agree with you, but unfortunately, it's pretty impossible to prove in court."

Terri studied his face. "Okay, spill. I know you well enough that I can tell when you're bothered by something. Stop telling me it's nothing or giving me bits and pieces. We said no secrets. We love each other, right?"

Max sighed. Loving Terri was new, and old habits

died hard. He'd been a survivor, leaning on no one but his family for far too long to simply turn over a new leaf without some setbacks. But he had promised Terri.

"After I rejected her yesterday, Lola threatened to take me to court and prove I'm an unfit father."

Terri's jaw dropped. "Surely she's joking. She can't mean that. No judge would ever believe you aren't a wonderful parent. How can she even *think* of doing such a thing?"

"I don't know. Lola's always overdramatic. But I can't take any chances. I've scheduled a meeting with my lawyer. I'll see him Monday afternoon and hear what he has to say."

Terri reached forward and stroked his cheek. "That sounds like a good idea. I'm sorry this is happening. You don't deserve this."

"Me, too. I just don't want to lose you."

Her touch was tender and reassuring. "You won't. I'm not going anywhere, I promise. Lola won't scare me away."

"That's good to know," Max replied. His heart overflowed. He lifted his finger and traced Terri's lips. Then he placed both hands on each side of her face and drew her mouth to his.

He kissed her long and hard, conveying through his touch how much he loved her. His breath mingled with hers and he leaned her back on the couch. This was his woman. "We'll take this one step at a time," he told her.

"We'll deal with everything as it comes," Terri promised. She leaned up to kiss him again.

"Exactly." And with that, Max let himself go.

CHAPTER FOURTEEN

"WHAT DO YOU MEAN there's no guarantee the judge won't rule in Lola's favor? How could I end up with less than I have now?" Max stared at his lawyer. If he hadn't known Reggie for years, he would have sworn that at this moment the man was crazy. No way could a judge seriously increase Lola's custody or even think about changing it completely.

"I thought once Mandy was twelve she got to have a say in where she lives," Max pointed out.

"She gets a say," Reggie said with a nod. "Mandy can speak with the judge and express her preferences and her thoughts on the custody arrangements. The meeting would be held in the judge's chambers without anyone else present."

"Makes sense," Max said. "So let's do that. Get a hearing scheduled."

"Not wise. That's a tactic for later. At this point I suggest not reopening anything and letting Lola make the first move."

"But you said Mandy can make her wishes known."

Reggie nodded. "Yes. But even if Mandy speaks with the judge, that doesn't mean the judge will do what she wants."

"This situation is ridiculous." Max's frustration mounted. He gazed at the law books on a shelf behind Reggie's oversize desk, a requisite in every law office.

It was Monday afternoon. Max had flown back from New Hampshire with Jim Latimer, leaving Terri to drive back herself. He hadn't liked leaving her, but she said she'd been driving her motor home for years.

"I just don't see how this could happen."

"Child custody is never simple," Reggie said. "I've seen cases I thought were sewn up go in the total opposite direction."

"That's not encouraging. I can't believe Lola can disrupt our lives like this. Surely the fact that she's never around will work in my favor."

"Most likely, but again, not guaranteed. The worst-case scenario is that Mandy moves in with her mother full-time. I doubt that will happen, but still, we have to consider the probability that the judge could order a fifty-fifty custody split now that Lola's back in Charlotte. That means Mandy would live half the week with you and half with Lola."

"That's an insane arrangement."

Reggie's expression remained sympathetic. "It's becoming very common across the country. Personally, I feel it's not in the best interest of the child, but it's actually been pushed for by dads who only get to see their children on weekends and want something more equitable."

"Yeah, except in this case *I* have primary physical custody and have had for all of Mandy's life. I'm not giving that up now."

"I hope you won't have to. The fact you've raised Mandy her entire life while Lola can't seem to decide

where to live and flits in and out of Charlotte should
weigh heavily in your favor. But the courts can be tricky.
I hate being cynical, but many times I think they do
more *in*justice than justice."

"So you're telling me I have little recourse except to
fight if Lola decides to follow through on her threats?"
Max didn't like this news one bit.

"We hope we don't have to go to trial, but if she files
to modify the custody agreement, we'll have to start the
legal haranguing. I doubt she'll be able to prove you're
an unfit parent. That's as hard as having the courts
declare someone incompetent. It's pretty rare."

"That's a relief." At least there was *some* good news.

"Most of the cases like this are heard in the family
court, and Judge Damschroader is hard to read. She's
made a lot of those 'live half-here, half-there' deci-
sions lately."

"Great," Max said. "This is not what I wanted to hear."

"I know, and I wish I could give you absolutes. It would
make my job a lot easier if I could. Unfortunately I can't
and I'll at least be up-front and honest with you about that."

"So what I am going to do?" Max asked.

Reggie leaned forward. "My advice to you is to wait.
Don't make any move until Lola does. She'll need to file
a motion to modify. Until that happens, keep the status
quo. She could be bluffing. I'd also advise you to track
her time with Mandy. Does she show up on time? That
kind of thing."

Max exhaled. "She's never on time. This past
weekend she left Mandy alone or with her grandmother
for most of the weekend and disappeared."

"Write all that down. From here on out, be on your guard and document, document, document."

"What about Terri? Do I have to stop seeing her like Lola insists? She thinks Terri's a bad influence."

"Does Terri do drugs? Any illegal activities? Does she cheat on her taxes?"

"No!" Max's reaction was instantaneous.

"Then you don't have anything to worry about there," Reggie reassured him. "It's natural for you to date. You told me you're not having her spend the night when Mandy's there, and when you're at the track you and Mandy sleep in the living area. I don't see any impropriety and doubt a judge will, either. You're allowed to move on with your life."

"Lola's really up in arms about Mandy being around her."

"I think you'll be fine. Again, just document everything. Try to keep Terri and Lola separated. There's no need for them to go out for tea or anything."

"Lola's already shown up where Terri works," Max said.

Reggie shook his head. "That's ballsy. Tell Terri to call the police if Lola does that again and have her escorted out if necessary."

Max sighed. "Thanks. I'll keep you posted."

Reggie gave Max a comforting smile. "That's what I'm here for."

"I know. We've been through a lot together."

"And we'll get through this one, too. Call me the minute Lola does anything or if you receive anything written from her lawyer."

"I will." When Max left the office he was still upset. He found himself faced with a variety of disturbing variables, with a good probability that things could take a turn in an unfavorable direction if he got the wrong judge.

At least the lawyer had indicated Max should keep seeing Terri. He had no desire to lose her or let her out of his life. But Lola…

As Max drove back to his office, he had no clue what would happen.

"SO HOW ARE THINGS going with you?" Bart asked Terri the Tuesday afternoon following his eighth-place finish in New Hampshire.

Today Terri had been going a bit easy on him, which meant she'd had him run only three miles, instead of three and a half. Bart'd had his weekly meeting with team owner Jim Latimer earlier that morning, and he'd reported that Jim was pleased the team and Bart had achieved four top-ten finishes in a row.

"Things are going okay," Terri said.

"You don't seem too happy," Bart observed.

"Max's ex-wife is causing problems. She decided she wanted to put her family back together, and Max said no."

"Good for him," Bart said.

"Yeah. Now that it's not going to happen, she's threatening Max with all sorts of legal action. He saw a lawyer yesterday, but I haven't yet talked to him to find out how it went. He's been in meetings all day and I didn't get home from New Hampshire until late last night."

"This Lola sounds like a real piece of work," Bart said, reaching for a sweat towel.

"Pretty much. She's a bit like Alyssa, only without the stardom."

"People, thankfully, have gotten a little tired of Alyssa. Now that her books are out, she's starting to become old news."

"That's a pretty upbeat attitude you have," Terri complimented him.

"Yeah, well, I'm in the Chase, my boss is happy and my mom's said she might come to a race."

"That's great. I know how you've missed her," Terri said. Bart stepped off the treadmill and Terri pointed to the elliptical. "Five minutes on here."

Bart climbed on. "So why don't you just marry Max? What could Lola do custody-wise if you did? You'd be a happy mom-and-pop household. How's she going to discredit that?"

"I don't know if Max and I are ready to get married. You know how well my engagement worked out with Harry. Max and I haven't been very successful in the wedding department. And it's not right to get married just so his ex-wife can't play dirty."

"Do you love Max?"

"Yes, but there's a difference between loving someone and committing the rest of your life to him. That's like you thinking my dad will be your crew chief for the rest of your racing career. He might, but in reality he probably won't. At some point he'll retire, like my mom wants him to."

"Yeah, but that's business. I still believe in true love, even though what my parents had turned out to be a sham. My sister has it. My younger brother Sawyer's found it. So maybe you've found it, too. It's nothing to be afraid of."

"Spoken like a man who has no fear of anything," Terri said. "That's why you might become a champion and I couldn't get myself out of the truck series. Just look at Max's divorce. Getting married takes thirty minutes. Getting divorced and dealing with the fallout takes years."

"But that doesn't mean you shouldn't consider marriage. Eventually that's where we all hope meaningful relationships end up. I'd like to be married someday, you know, to a woman who knows that driving is really important to me but still loves me for what's inside, not for what I do."

"You surprise me sometimes with how deep and insightful you are," Terri said.

"That's me, Mr. Sensitive. A big teddy bear, only not so soft around the middle anymore."

"Well, get off that machine and get back over here to the bench press," Terri told him. "I'll toughen you up."

Bart moved and positioned himself on his back. He gazed up at Terri. "What?" she asked.

"Seriously, you really got to get this hang-up of yours dealt with," he urged.

"I don't have any hang-ups," Terri insisted.

"Yeah, you do. You've already committed your heart to the guy, so why are you hesitating? It's like getting in the car to race. You gotta be ready to go the distance, especially if the prize at the end is worth it."

She paused. "I never thought of it that way."

"Yeah, well, I'm not sure where that came from.

Probably from me trying to get my mom back out in the world and at the race track. But I'm right." He gazed at her pointedly.

"You are and you suck," Terri told him with an exaggerated sigh.

"So I don't have to do these?" he asked, trying to wriggle out of his exercises.

"Good try, but it's not going to work. You've still got five more of those to do."

Bart was right, she admitted later, once she'd returned to her cottage to shower and change before meeting Max and Mandy. This relationship had permanence written all over it, especially once they'd declared their love.

If she really loved Max, she'd want a future with him, and since he was a traditional guy, that future meant marriage. He'd made her break all her rules. He normally wasn't what she looked for in a man. But he fit her perfectly and she loved being with him.

The big variable in the equation was Lola and her threats. She should be able to let go and move on.

Lola had made Max paranoid. For a brief second a vise gripped Terri's heart. What if Max didn't change his mind about marriage? What if he meant what he said, that he never planned to remarry? Where would that leave her? Despite her own reservations about marriage, Terri wanted what her parents shared.

Her phone rang as she stepped out of the shower. In her hurry to answer, she didn't look at the number. "Hey."

"Hey right back at you, babe. Never had you greet me that way before."

Bonds. "I thought you were someone else."

Her agent chuckled. "And here I finally thought that breathy voice was just for me." He made a tsking sound of disappointment and jumped into his spiel. "Need you in L.A. on Thursday. One-day job. Company wants to update that commercial you did a few years ago with the new car, which is actually the car of today, I guess. They need you to drive some laps in Fontana. Pretty basic stuff for you. Did you get that new vehicle?"

"I did. Broke down and got an SUV. But I bought a hybrid." She readjusted her towel.

"I've already got your plane booked and am e-mailing you your itinerary. I'll have a car meet you at LAX and drive you everywhere where you need to be. Have you back home on the red-eye."

"You know I hate flying the red-eye," she told him.

"Yeah, but don't you have to make a drive to Dover this weekend?"

"You know me far too well," she said.

"That's my little moneymaker. We'll do dinner the next time you're out here. I hear there's another racing film working its way up the pipe at one of the big studios. I think you're going to be a star."

"No one ever sees my face, remember?"

"But they'll see you drive and, baby, you can certainly do that," Bonds replied before hanging up.

Terri finished getting ready and drove to Max's. "Hi," he said, kissing her the moment she got in the front door. "I've missed you."

"Me, too," Terri said, letting herself memorize the feel of his lips.

"I'm finishing up dinner."

"You're cooking?"

He laughed at her worried expression. "Okay, you caught me. I'm reheating. Gourmet dinner already prepared for two."

"So where's Mandy?"

"She's at my mom's. I figured we needed a little alone time. We haven't had that since this weekend."

She drew him into her arms. "Then why are we wasting time? Eating food can wait."

They ate about an hour and a half later.

"This is good," Terri told him as she tried the salmon.

"The supermarket has these awesome meals-to-go. They've allowed Mandy and me to eat fresh food, instead of frozen pizza all the time. They market it as 'having your own personal chef.'"

Terri took a bite of the saffron-and-almond rice. "They've sold me. This is delicious."

They ate for a few more minutes, discussing mundane things until Terri finally broached the subject of Lola. "So what did the lawyer say yesterday?"

"You want the good or the bad news?" Max asked.

"Both," Terri said.

"The good news is that Lola really doesn't have a chance of getting me declared an unfit father. My lawyer's very confident on that point. He also said that it doesn't matter if she hates you, unless you're some strung-out drug addict or engaged in illegal activities, there's no reason for me to stop dating you to appease her misguided sensibilities."

Relief flowed through Terri. She'd been worried Lola could force Max's hand. "Good."

"It is good. I'm not ready for you to go anywhere," Max said.

"Me, neither. So things can be normal."

"Or as much as they can be with Lola acting up."

"We can deal with that. And just so you know, I'll be shooting another commercial Thursday. I'm going to fly out really early and come back on the red-eye. Then it's off to Dover for the three of us."

"Sounds great. I'm looking forward to getting out of here for the weekend. I really enjoy being at the track. It's a huge stress reliever."

"Yeah, those hard cards and flying on private jets can be pretty addicting," Terri said.

He grinned. "You know what I mean. I sit behind a desk or a conference table most of the day. It's great to be outside and experience the rumble and roar of the engines. Awesome, in fact. It's like a mini-vacation every weekend. And I love being with you. I'm not going to let Lola ruin what we have."

"Thank you." His declaration meant everything. "I just can't stand how she treats you and Mandy. There has to be something that can be done."

"Here's the bad news. My lawyer said that reopening the child-custody agreement could be risky. I could lose more than I gain." Max filled Terri in on everything Reggie had said.

"That's just wrong," Terri replied when he'd finished.

Max covered her hand with his. "I know. It'll also get expensive and drag on, and no one will benefit from it. But Lola's unreasonable. She broke all our wedding crystal in a fit of rage. She's a mess. Always has been.

But she's Mandy's mother, for better or worse. I wish that were different."

Terri hesitated and then said, "Bart thinks we should just get married."

Max dropped his fork, he was so shocked by her words. "Married?" He fumbled as he retrieved the utensil.

"There's not much Lola could do if we were married," Terri went on.

"She could still demand fifty percent of Mandy's time. Meaning that Mandy would have to live with her. Marriage isn't something you rush into or do for the wrong reason. I did that before, remember?"

"I didn't say it was my idea," Terri said. "Bart thought of it."

"If marriage is in our future, we'll know when the time is right. I don't want us to lose sight of why we're together, which is that we *choose* to be. It's not because we have some piece of paper saying we must. Fifty percent of couples get divorced. I don't want to be there ever again."

"I can understand," Terri said, trying not to tremble. Even after breaking off her engagement, she figured she'd know when she'd met Mr. Right.

Wasn't that the irony? She finally wanted commitment, but she'd fallen in love with someone who'd been burned by it.

"You've grown quiet," Max stated.

"I'm thinking about what you just said. I guess Bart's dad is an example of what you mean. He stayed in a marriage and kept a mistress because of finances. It's sad."

"Exactly," Max said. "I don't think marriage makes

things better. It often makes it worse. That's why you didn't marry Harry. You realized it was all wrong for you."

"I guess."

Max placed his hand over hers and lifted it to his lips. "You mean the world to me. So, Dover?" he asked, changing the subject.

She nodded, unsettled by his casual dismissal of the topic. "Yeah. You'll like the track. It's a one-mile concrete oval. The NASCAR Nationwide and NASCAR Sprint Cup garages are at opposite ends of the track. We'll be attending both races. Average speed will be about 120."

"Sounds great," Max said, and Terri managed to be upbeat and happy until Mandy arrived home. But deep down she remained troubled by their conversation. Their relationship had a crack in it now, at least on her side.

"Hi, Terri!" Mandy said as she bounded in, Max's mother on her heels. Max stood and gave his mother a hug.

"What's up?" Mandy asked Terri.

Terri watched as Mandy stowed her backpack. "Not much. I'm flying to California to shoot a commercial on Thursday, but it's only a one-day trip."

"Cool. So we're on for Dover, right?" Mandy asked.

Terri nodded. "Yep. I won't go to Kansas or the last three races, but I plan to be at the rest."

"Can I go to some of them? I don't want to go to Mom's every weekend. Last time was so boring. And lately she's always on the phone talking to people all hush-hush. We don't go anywhere anymore."

"We'll have to see what your mom says. She's actually saying that she wants to spend more time with you," Max told his daughter.

Mandy huffed. "I don't believe that for a minute."

"At least she's around for your birthday," Max pointed out.

"*This* year," Mandy said, rolling her eyes. "I told Lynn I'd call her when I got home." She headed for her bedroom.

"She's not been very happy lately," Max's mother, Jean, said. Terri had met her a few times already and liked her. "Something's going on over at Lola's."

"There's always something going on," Max said with a shrug. "That's just the nature of the beast called Lola."

"Still, it seems like it's something more this time," his mother said, and then with a quick kiss to Max's cheek, she left for home.

"I should probably go, too," Terri told Max. "You've got to make sure Mandy's homework is done and that she's for ready for school in the morning. It's also your reality-TV-show night."

"You could stay and watch with us," Max offered.

Terri shook her head. "Nope. That's your and Mandy's special time. I used to love when it was just me and my dad out in his race shop. Those are some of my fondest memories. Go. She'll be grown before you know it."

His face turned wistful. "She already is. It seems like yesterday I was buckling her up into her car seat. Now she's three years away from driving her own car."

"Exactly," Terri said. She helped Max clear the plates, do the dishes and then she kissed him goodbye. "I'll call you tomorrow or you call me."

"Deal," Max said. He kissed her now, letting his lips linger on hers. Then Terri headed out and started her SUV. The headlights cut a swath through the darkness.

She turned her radio off, letting the silence build. Frustration consumed her.

She no longer wanted fun and fancy-free. She wanted commitment, the entire package. The moment was a revelation. She didn't feel like she was about to face a firing squad. She wasn't afraid.

But Max was. And she didn't know if he could change.

CHAPTER FIFTEEN

THURSDAY FOUND Terri in sunny Southern California. The premise behind the commercial was simple: one "bad" soft-drink company was trying to spy on its competitor's consumers to find out why they liked the other brand best. The "good" soda company didn't mind, because in the end, the bad company realized its product would never be better.

How they would manage to take the spy theme and work it into a racing commercial baffled Terri, but she did what she was paid to do, which was drive a few laps at high speed, creep the car through the infield like she was spying, and then do a few takes on the highway that the production crew had arranged to have shut down.

Terri hadn't worked with this particular director before, but Bonds had assured her the man knew his stuff. From the director's use of toy cars to map out the scene, she could tell the guy had a pretty good grasp of what he wanted.

She'd film a chase sequence next with a cop car—how one of those could catch a stock car was again something beyond her comprehension. She'd long ago given up trying to understand the editing part of the process and simply enjoyed how the commercial turned out when she finally saw it on television.

She had, however, worked with the guy who'd be driving the police car, and she laughed and joked with him as they waited for their cue to climb in and get started.

"So, you hear about that upcoming racing movie?" he asked.

"Yeah. Do you know what it's about?" Unlike her, he lived in L.A. and so had his finger on the pulse of the town gossip and industry news.

"My agent says it's a combination of a love story and a spy thriller set in the world of stock car racing. Something to do with how the series now goes out of the country."

"Yeah, the NASCAR Nationwide Series races in Mexico and Canada. But those are our allies."

He shrugged. "I have no idea how the plot is going to work. Maybe there's a fuel shortage. Or a plot to fill the haulers with explosives and try to get them back across the border or something. You know writers. They'll figure it all out somehow."

His cell phone rang and he held up a finger. "Hold on. Gotta take this." He moved a few feet away and listened. "Okay. Yeah. No, I need you to do this. I'm on a shoot. Get the zoom lens and follow her. Her husband wants to know everyone she's meeting."

"Sorry about that," he said, closing his phone.

"Speaking of a spy thriller—a zoom lens? A wayward wife? What's that about?"

He grinned. "I moonlight as a private eye to help pay the bills. Let me tell you, the job's not as glamorous as it is in the movies. Mostly it involves sitting in a lot of really hot stuffy cars waiting for hours for one sighting. But you'd be amazed how busy we are. Everyone in L.A. thinks his spouse is cheating."

"Huh," Terri said, her curiosity piqued. "So what else does a private eye do when not on stakeout?"

"Lots of computer work. We can track just about anyone. Their financials. Their credit history. Where they eat and shop. Job history, which in this town is important, as people like to pad their acting résumé."

"Really?" Terri asked. "So you can get all that information?"

He shrugged. "Pretty much. The Internet's a great tool, and I've got access to a lot of servers and databases the average American doesn't even know exist."

Terri found this fascinating. "So if I gave you a name, you could…" She paused, figuring he'd fill in the rest, which he did.

"I could basically give you the activities of that person's life for the past few years," he told her.

"What if I wanted them followed? I assume from your earlier conversation you do that."

He nodded. "Yes, here in L.A. If you wanted someone followed who lives in San Francisco, for example, I might bring someone in from up there who'd be a little more familiar with the lay of the city, that kind of thing. The agency I work for has a network of other reputable agencies. Some private eyes are just incompetent. Others are quite good and even do things such as personal security and risk management."

"I never would have known. So what does a private

eye cost?" Terri asked, her mind racing as she considered the possibilities.

"It depends on the services you want. A background check is usually pretty reasonable. We can do that from a desk. A basic investigation will go a lot higher."

"How high?" Terri asked. "Say for an entire weekend. With pictures and video."

"I'd say you're talking about in the mid-four figures. It's not cheap. Why? Do you have someone you want followed?"

Terri nodded. "I just might. My boyfriend's ex-wife is making life miserable for us. She's taking their daughter for her weekend visits, but disappearing. I'd like some ammunition of my own."

"That's usually a good thing in cases like this," he said. "I could set you up with someone in your hometown. That way all I'll get is a referral fee. You don't want to pay me and have me turn around and subcontract out the job."

That was for sure. She wasn't made of money. "No, unfortunately I'm not that wealthy. But this shoot was unplanned, so I can use my newfound riches to help foot the bill."

"Yeah." He laughed, knowing the general amount they were both making for today's job.

"But it would have to be very discreet. I can't risk anyone knowing what I'm doing, and that includes my boyfriend," Terri continued.

"You won't even need to meet with the private investigator. It can all be done over the phone and the package mailed or couriered to you."

"Amazing," she said, feeling the mild depression she'd been experiencing since Tuesday lift somewhat. She'd do this for Max. He deserved happiness. However, she wasn't certain how he'd take her actions, so for now he could remain in the dark. She did feel a bit guilty since she'd insisted on them having no secrets. She'd tell him as soon as the job was done, she promised herself. Sometimes the ends justified the means, and she would trust her instincts that this was one of those cases.

"So do you want me to set you up?" he asked.

"Hey, you two! We're ready! Get in the cars!" a production assistant yelled.

Terri made her decision. "Yes, I do."

"Great. I'll do it as soon as I chase you down and we get done filming."

She gave him a wink and grinned. "That's if you can catch me. I do believe the director said I'm supposed to win."

He laughed at that, and soon they were on their way.

Later that evening, with the matter settled and a Charlotte investigative firm already on the case, Terri slept the entire flight home.

BY THE TIME she, Max and Mandy arrived in Dover early Saturday morning, Terri was feeling better about her decision. Lola was one of those women with whom you needed to fight fire with fire.

Terri had no problems handling fire. But for today and tomorrow, she planned on enjoying herself with the people she cared about.

Her dad was in the garage area, up to his elbows in

grease and grime, when she caught up with him. She gave him a quick kiss on the cheek.

"We have to change the engine," he told her. "This one blew up during practice. It's like Bart overdrove it, but I watched him and that's not what happened."

"It's a minor setback. You've handled worse," Terri soothed.

"Yeah, hopefully, but as we've already qualified we'll be starting from the back of the pack," Philip replied. "It's not a position I wanted to be in."

"It'll be okay, Dad," Terri said, and she left her father alone with his team and his thoughts.

She, Max and Mandy had developed a pattern at the tracks they visited. If there was a NASCAR Nationwide Series race, they'd watch that. Evenings they'd hang out in the Drivers' and Owners' lot and spend time together, either playing board games or video games. Then everyone would crash.

The next morning, while Terri gave Bart his workout, Max and Mandy explored the outside of the track, including souvenir row. Mandy had started bringing back collectibles from each track, something for her and something for Lynn. Mandy's goal was to find something track-specific. The plan for the afternoon was watching the NASCAR Sprint Cup Series race. Terri had secured seats in an air-conditioned part of the grandstand.

Despite starting at the back of the pack, Bart managed to get himself up to thirteenth place when the checkered flag flew. His brother Will had come in tenth, and sandwiched between them was Justin Murphy at twelfth position. Leaving Dover, Dean Grosso led the

Chase for the NASCAR Sprint Cup points, followed by his son, Kent, in second.

Will sat at eleventh, and Bart had moved from tenth at the beginning of the Chase to sixth following this race. All in all, not a bad place to be, for there were still a few races left.

If Bart and her father could eke out some wins, and if Dean and Kent saw some terrible finishes, the Chase standings could change dramatically. Of course, Hart Hampton, Rafael O'Bryan and Justin Murphy were still ahead of Bart, as well.

Since the race was an afternoon event, Max and Mandy would accompany Terri on the eight-hour drive back to Charlotte. By a little after five, they were on their way. Mandy had slept in Terri's bed for the last part of the journey since she had school in the morning. They'd stop for dinner along the way.

"You know, I'm glad we did this," Max said. He'd moved to the front of the motor home for a second.

"What? Dover?" Terri asked.

"No, us."

His words were sweet and caused her to feel all warm and tingly. "Me, too," Terri replied.

"You two are being sappy again!" Mandy yelled from the sofa.

"Put your headphones on for a few minutes," her dad called back.

"All right," Mandy said.

"You will have to go sit down," Terri told him.

"I know. But I just wanted you to know."

"Thanks," she said, always appreciative of Max's

little gestures. She accelerated, needing to exit and change highways. Max returned to the living area, out of sight behind her. Terri focused on the road.

THE PACKAGE ARRIVED via courier at Terri's studio by noon on Tuesday. Nothing about the nondescript, padded brown envelope revealed that the contents contained anything exceptional.

Terri's fingers trembled, however, as she pulled the strip and opened the envelope. From the interior she drew out a spiral-bound dossier complete with CD-ROM and a file folder containing several eight-by-ten color photos. She pulled those out first, seeing shots of Lola leaving a motel room with an older man, his arm around her. Other photos showed them cozying up at dinner, the man going so far as to feed Lola a chocolate-covered strawberry.

Terri winced at the seductive look in Lola's eyes. This was not the demeanor of a woman who'd declared she wanted to get her ex-husband back; this was a woman bent on seducing the guy in front of her. From the expression on his face, Lola was doing a darn fine job. On the back of each photo was a descriptive caption and a time/date stamp. The man was Jeremy Jones, a Hollywood producer.

She placed the photos back inside the file folder and opened the dossier. She skimmed over Lola's financials, as well as information about Jeremy Jones. The report indicated he'd left his wife six months ago and was currently in the middle of a nasty divorce. Jeremy's production company had produced a string of box office successes over the past ten years, including one of the top-grossing movies of last year.

Terri had seen the film, and she had to admit the action-adventure piece was worthy of the Oscar nod it had received.

Terri found the entire scenario very interesting. She didn't exactly know how to handle a situation like this, but she knew the man who would. She reached for the phone and called Bonds.

CHAPTER SIXTEEN

"HI, TERRI. Sorry I missed you. I have the best news. Can we see each other tonight? I want to tell you in person. I love you."

Terri listened to the voice mail one more time, letting the feeling of warmth she always got from hearing Max's voice steal over her. She hated that she'd missed his call, but once she'd called Bonds, she had a better idea of how to proceed.

Terri pressed a button on her keypad, playing Max's message for a third time. His voice had sounded excited, almost giddy. Something was up.

She wished he'd given her a clue to the nature of his good news, but whatever it was, she could tell he was in a great mood.

Terri tapped the envelope the investigator had sent. She'd stuffed everything back inside, including the notes she'd jotted while speaking with Bonds.

Yeah, having Lola investigated could be seen as a little underhanded. And Max was such an upright guy. But sometimes a little information was a powerful thing.

MAX HADN'T BEEN able to get out of work until his normal time, even though he'd skipped lunch. He still couldn't believe what had happened. He wished he'd gotten through to Terri, but he'd see her a little later. He couldn't wait to tell her.

It seemed like Lady Luck was finally on his side. First he'd met Terri, and now his job had come through in the biggest way.

The only downer was Lola, but for today he refused to think about her.

"So what's your news?" his mom asked when Max entered the kitchen. Needing to share with someone, he'd called her earlier, but she'd not answered, either, so he'd decided to go to her place.

He'd had a silly grin on his face all day and he didn't lose it now. "I got promoted."

"Really?" This jubilant shout came from his daughter. "Does that mean I can have that new iPod I want?"

"We'll see. Your birthday is around the corner, and my raise is effective as of next week. I also get a new office, and a new job. I'm now in the PR department permanently. One of my main accounts…all Rocksolid's NASCAR relations!"

His mind boggled at how things had occurred. He'd been called into an unscheduled executive meeting. By the end, he'd been promoted to PR overseeing NASCAR and others, and reporting to Alan Henson. He even had a staff to supervise.

"That's great!" Mandy said. She stood and gave her dad a hug, and then she pulled back and looked up at him. "What's that mean?"

"In terms of NASCAR, it means that my favorite driver will be Billy Budd as he's the guy Rocksolid sponsors."

"He's not so bad. He's actually closing in on rookie of the year. One sports announcer said if he lives up to what he did this season he'll be a driver to watch for in years to come," Mandy said.

"Well, that's what we're hoping," Max replied. His stomach grumbled.

"There's still some meat loaf and mashed potatoes left," his mother said.

The clock on the oven displayed a few minutes before six, meaning Max had time to grab a quick bite. "I think I'll have a plate. I do have to leave soon. I've asked Terri to meet me at the house. I want to tell her the news."

"Now you can afford to buy her a ring," Mandy informed him. "After my iPod."

"A ring?" Max asked as his mother served him a plate of food. He'd pop in the den and tell his dad the news once he finished eating. His father never liked to be interrupted while the news was on.

"Yep. A ring. You *are* going to marry her eventually, aren't you, Dad?" Mandy pressed.

"We've only been dating a couple of months," Max said.

"So?"

Max ate some potatoes to keep from replying immediately. "I care about Terri very much."

"So marry her. I like her. Lynn thinks she's cool. If you're married, then I can bring Lynn with me to the track, instead of waiting until the races come back to Charlotte in a few weeks."

"Why can't Lynn come now?" Jean asked.

"Because Dad's not married and she'd have to sleep out in the living room with us."

"She stays over here," Max said, puzzled.

"Yeah, in my room. It's a bit creepy to have a friend sleeping in the same room with you and your dad. Yuck. I mean, even if you do wear real clothes to sleep in."

Max had to agree with her, so he nodded.

"And if you and Terri get married, you two can share a bed, and Lynn and I can have the front." Mandy had it all worked out. "So marry Terri. I like her and she makes you happy."

"It's not that simple sometimes," Max said, starting on the meat loaf and wondering how this conversation had gotten out of hand.

"Yes, it is. You buy a ring and ask her to marry you. She says yes, and then you both say I do and I wear a dress and be a bridesmaid."

Sensing Max's conundrum and his need to be alone with his daughter, Max's mom left the room.

"Honey," Max began, "I don't know if Terri and I are ready for marriage. We both have our careers. Even if we did get married, she's not going to stay home and be like Lynn's mom."

"I know that," Mandy shot back. "Get with the times, Dad."

"Okay, then," Max said, leaning back in his chair. He was a bit confused. When did young girls get so smart?

"So if I'm okay with Terri working, I don't know why you can't marry her."

"She and I will have to talk about it," he said, giving

his daughter the only answer he could. He and Terri hadn't even discussed living together.

"It's really simple. You buy her flowers and get down on one knee," Mandy said.

"That's the movies. It's a little more complicated than that in real life."

Max was fast losing ground. How did one break it to a child that the idea of marriage scared him? Terri had already ended one engagement. What if they got engaged and then it fell apart? Max couldn't handle the hurt for himself, much less see his daughter go through it. He knew Terri wasn't ready, either—at least, he didn't think so. She hadn't told him any different, had she?

"Did you eat enough dinner?" Max asked Mandy as she began to pack up her homework.

"Yeah. Grandma made it a little differently this time. It wasn't so bad once I put ketchup on it."

The meat loaf was actually moist and delicious. He'd bring Terri some. He knew her well enough to know she probably hadn't eaten dinner.

He glanced at the clock. He'd given Terri a key to his house. If she arrived before seven and he wasn't there, she'd assume he was picking up Mandy and use her key. Thus, still wanting to talk to his daughter, Max stood and refilled his plate.

THE LIGHTS WERE OFF at Max's when Terri arrived. Whatever he'd been excited about had to be huge, and she'd felt a fission of disappointment she'd beaten him home. She used her key and entered, flipping on light switches as she went.

She sat down in front of the television and dialed him before she turned the set on. "Hey," she said, when she got ahold of him. "I'm here at your place."

"I'm getting in the car now. My mom made meat loaf and I'm bringing you some."

"Sounds great. I'll see you in a few," Terri replied, disconnecting. Max's mom only lived about ten minutes away.

About seven minutes later she heard a car drive up, and she muted the television. No garage door opened and, instead, the front doorbell rang. She gazed through the peephole and grimaced.

"I know you're standing there!" Lola yelled. "Your car is in the driveway. Let me in."

Against her better judgment, Terri complied. "Hello, Lola."

"You'd better not be living here now," Lola stated as she stepped inside.

Terri readied herself for battle. "I'm not, but I have a key."

Lola's eyes narrowed. "Where's Max?"

"On his way. He should be here any minute. He had to get Mandy. He's bringing me dinner."

"Does his mother still do meat loaf every Tuesday? How boring," Lola said, her gaze traveling around the room. "I want to talk to Max, so why don't you leave before he gets here? I'll explain where you've gone."

"Not going to happen," Terri said evenly.

"You're making a big mistake," Lola said. "Do you know who I am?"

"Do you know who *I* am?" Terri countered easily.

"I'm Max's girlfriend. His future. You are his past. I would suggest you leave him alone. It's over, Lola."

She scowled. "I'm not going to do that. We share a daughter we both love a great deal. That bond will always be between us and it will bring us back together."

"Why do you want him back?" Terri demanded. "What is it that you suddenly see in him after all this time?" She planted her hands on her hips. "You showed no interest in the man for ten years. Now, when he's serious about someone, you suddenly have a change of heart and insist that he's yours? Were you one of those people who didn't like your toys but demanded them back when some other kid wanted to play with them? You can't have all the men you set your sights on bow down before you."

"Max loves me. He always has. I've been the only woman for him."

"Until now." Terri's tone was deadly quiet. "Now I'm the only woman for him. And you need to realize that and move on. You need to stop deluding yourself."

"I'm not!" Lola shouted.

"Yes, you are. Worse, you're not even serious about him." Terri reached forward and grabbed the envelope off the table. She'd brought it so she could tell Max what she'd done. And while this was not the plan she and Bonds had discussed, Terri was angry. She tossed the package at Lola. She had another one like it at home. "Go ahead. Open it."

Lola's fingers fumbled with removing the contents, and her eyes widened with horror when she saw the pictures. "You…you…you…"

An expletive burst forth from Lola's mouth, but Terri didn't stop. "What did you plan to do, Lola? Keep a rich married guy on the side? For someone who's trying to win back Max's heart, I wouldn't think sleeping with some other man is the way to do it. And you had the nerve to tell Max you would have him declared an unfit father."

"I can't believe you…" Lola rattled off another string of colorful curses. Terri stood there and endured the insults. They couldn't hurt her.

"Max will be home soon," Terri said as Lola's tirade seemed to wind down.

"Actually—" Max's voice cut through the room like a knife "—I've been standing here the entire time."

CHAPTER SEVENTEEN

MAX HAD KNOWN there was trouble the moment he'd turned onto his street and seen Lola's car out front and Terri's in the driveway. That was simply a recipe for disaster, and the loud voices arguing inside the living room were an indication he'd been correct. Luckily Mandy had been wearing her earphones and so had been oblivious to the argument ensuing in the other room. He'd sent her into the kitchen with the meat loaf and gone to stop the fray.

What he'd overheard had shocked him. Just like a professional football team could score a touchdown in less than thirty seconds, he'd learned a lot of shocking information in a few short seconds.

He'd planned to step forward and stop the fight before Mandy returned and found her mother in a fit of rage. Now he understood the reasons, and he worked to check his own anger.

"Max." Lola gave him her best high-wattage smile. "Your girlfriend is trying to smear my good name."

"I'm sure you managed just fine on your own," Max replied. To find out Lola was having sex with another man while professing to want him back proved her intentions were as phony as a three-dollar bill.

While he hadn't wanted to rekindle anything with her, anyway, to find out she'd been plying him the entire time with falsehoods was a despicable low blow. Once again she'd used him.

"What did you hear?" Terri asked.

"Enough to know that Lola's been lying to me and playing me for a fool and that you hired someone to expose her lies," Max said. The high his promotion had given him was completely deflated.

"I'm sorry," Terri told him.

"We'll talk in a minute." He gazed at the paper all over the floor. "I assume these are the pictures."

"I have another set," Terri said. "The company I used sent me two and a complete dossier."

"You have a report on me?" Lola shrieked, and Max put his hand up.

"Lower your voice," he said and the edge in his tone had Lola closing her mouth. "I'd like to see those."

Terri nodded, but made no motion. She understood he meant later. "Mandy put your meat loaf in the kitchen. Do you mind waiting in there while I show Lola out?"

Terri nodded, then turned and left the room. Max faced his ex-wife.

"Don't even start," he stated flatly. "Just tell me, why did you do it? Why lie to me and pretend you want me back when you are obviously seeing someone else?"

"Because you've always loved me," she said.

Max shook his head. "No, I didn't. What we had was young love. It's not the kind that lasts or endures. I don't want what we had. You are not the woman for me.

Get that through your head. Whoever this guy is, he can have you. I'm done. Set your sights elsewhere."

"I don't know if he wants me," Lola wailed. "Not long-term. I don't want to be alone anymore."

And that was the problem, Max realized. His ex-wife had never grown up. She had to have someone want her, and she'd turned back to Max. He, however, had no problem being single.

"That's a problem you'll have to solve. But if he doesn't want you, find someone else. You need to leave me alone. I've said it before, but it bears repeating. You and I are finished."

"Fine. I'll go back to L.A. As long as your—" Lola managed to stifle whatever unpleasant term she had for Terri "—girlfriend doesn't show those pictures all over town or to her agent. That'd ruin me. Jerry would hate me. He's going through a divorce."

"That's his problem and yours. I'm not putting up with any more of your drama. You want those pictures quashed, then you're going to have to give me what I want."

"And what's that?" She eyed him suspiciously.

"Peace and quiet. No more threats. You and I will sign new papers granting me full legal custody of Mandy. Both primary and physical. You will contact me before you visit. I won't deny you seeing her, but you're not going to simply drop in and expect to pick up where you left off. Mandy's never been your priority."

"I love her."

"Then do what's right by her," Max said. He knew he sounded harsh, but he wasn't stopping until he protected his daughter's future. "Stop running to her and dragging her into your world. She's not some teddy bear you can cling to."

"I'm her mother." The waterworks had started and black mascara rivers coursed down Lola's cheeks.

"No one is saying you're not. But I want things finalized and finished. You will never threaten to take her away from me again."

"That's unfair," Lola accused.

Max didn't care what Lola thought. He just wanted to protect Mandy. Knowing that he could now have that absolute his lawyer couldn't guarantee...

"I'll call my lawyer first thing in the morning," he said. "You can expect paperwork within the week. Don't fight me on this."

It seemed the wind had finally gone out of Lola's sails. She shook her head. "I won't."

"Thank you." However, he'd believe it when it was over and done.

"I'll expect you to keep up your end of the bargain once we make it."

"So long as you adhere to yours, nothing will ever be made public," Max confirmed.

"Fine." Lola strode to the front door, her face a mess. "Give Mandy my love. Tell her I'll call her tomorrow. I do want to see her before her birthday."

"I'll tell her," Max replied. He took a deep breath once Lola's taillights disappeared from view. Hopefully, that was over with, settled.

Only time would tell, but it appeared Lola would be reasonable. She didn't want to see herself in tabloid hell. Maybe that was the start of a positive change. For everyone's sake.

Max strode into the kitchen. Mandy had disappeared into her bedroom and Terri only picked at the food in front of her, too upset to eat. "Hi," she said.

Max sank into the chair next to her. He winced when his next words came out like an accusation. "Hi. Were you planning on telling me about the photos?"

She glanced at her lap. "That's why I had them with me tonight."

"So you didn't want to ask me about this first?"

"I saw an opportunity and I took it. I had to move fast."

"We're not supposed to be keeping secrets from each other," Max said.

She lifted her gaze. "I thought I could help. Mandy mentioned her mother was going out and leaving her alone. While I was in California I found out one of the guys I was working with moonlights as a private eye. So I asked him for a referral and he got me set up."

"You should have told me. You should have asked me first. I've been handling myself and Lola for a long time."

"Yes, but that was before you met me," Terri replied with a frown.

"It doesn't change that she's my problem, not yours. I had it handled."

"I was only trying to help. I love you. That's what people in love do."

"You had no right. We've only been dating for a couple of months, if that. You overstepped."

Max knew if he could stand outside the situation and looked at it from afar, he'd probably slap himself upside the head and call himself an idiot for the way he was acting. But he couldn't distance himself enough at this moment to see logic. All he could do was feel. Both Terri and Lola had injured his pride.

Lola had only wanted him back because she didn't want to be alone. Terri hadn't trusted him enough to tell him about her plan or thought him able to handle Lola himself, as he'd been doing for years.

He needed time to think. He'd gone from an incredible high to a miserable low. All in the span of twenty minutes. "I really don't want to talk about this tonight," he said.

"Fine." Terri stood and put her plate in the sink.

"That's it?" he asked, surprised. She was leaving?

"Look, I don't know what news you had to share. I'm not sure what's going on with you. But whatever it is, I have a suspicion you need to work through the situation on your own. I'm going home. I'm sorry—what I did was wrong. I'll put the envelope containing everything by your back door. You call me when you're ready."

He hadn't meant for her to go. Okay, maybe he had. Tonight was like being on a roller coaster. Mandy wanted him to marry Terri. Max wasn't sure he was ready to let himself believe in happy endings, especially after what had just happened.

He glanced up, but Terri was gone.

"DAD, ISN'T TERRI going to join us?" Mandy asked as family members descended on the house for her birthday party. Since Max had to fly to Kansas the next morning, they were having the party Friday night.

"Terri's probably in Kansas," Max said, not wanting to reveal that the only contact he'd had with Terri since Tuesday had been two measly text messages. He'd tried to call her, but he hadn't yet gotten through. He'd left voice mails, but she'd so far failed to return his calls.

"She sent you a present," Max said, pointing to the box that had arrived in the mail yesterday. He'd been happy Terri hadn't forgotten his daughter.

"Yeah, but I'd kind of like to have her here with us," Mandy said.

"All your cousins are here." Max tried the bait-and-switch tactic. His brothers, their wives, his parents, everyone had showed for Mandy's official celebration of turning thirteen.

The only one absent was Lola, who had returned to L.A. that morning.

Thursday afternoon she'd brought her lawyer and he'd met with them in a conference room at Reggie's firm. Thanks to his lawyer and the information Terri had compiled, Max had in his hand the new custody agreement they'd hashed out. He'd gotten what he wanted, which was security for Mandy. The fact that he'd had it this fast was nothing short of miraculous. Terri's investigation had done the trick. He owed her for that.

Mandy hadn't seemed too surprised to learn her mother was leaving again. She'd grown up with Lola's vanishing act. The person she was looking for and asking about this weekend was Terri. Max's fear, that his daughter would become close to Terri and then Terri would walk out of his life, had become reality.

So he tried to enjoy himself, focusing on hanging out with his brothers and letting Mandy be the star of the weekend. She received some great gifts, but even after everyone had left late that night, she still hadn't unwrapped Terri's.

"You really should open that," he said.

Mandy shook her head. "I don't feel like it. Maybe she can come over Monday when she gets back. You are going to see her again, aren't you, Dad?"

A little piece of Max's heart broke. "I don't know," he told her.

"Do you love her?" Mandy asked.

"Yes, I do." Truer words were never spoken.

Mandy tilted her head. She was officially a teenager now, and he saw her as a young woman and no longer a child, especially when she said, "Does she love you?"

"I think so."

"Then what's the problem? Grandma says if you love someone, you should talk to that person and work it out."

"It's not that simple," Max said.

"You always say that. The counselor you sent me to—remember that time when I was younger?—said I'd work through how I felt. I finally realized Mom simply can't help being who she is."

"That's pretty mature of you," Max said.

"Yeah, well, I've been thinking about this a lot. I knew she'd never be like Lynn's mom. And back when I was little I wanted you and Mom to get back together."

"All kids want that. It's normal."

"Yes, but you wouldn't be happy because Mom would always feel trapped living in Charlotte. She needs stardom."

Max thought of the producer Lola had managed to semi-snag. "She does."

"You need Terri. You've been happy since you met her. Since Tuesday, even with your promotion you've been miserable. Will you please work things out? I can't stand you being sad."

Max drew his daughter into a hug. "I'll try," he promised.

"That's all I ask," Mandy said. She stepped out of his embrace and, leaving Terri's present, went to her bedroom.

Carrying the remaining plates to the dishwasher, Max began to straighten up the house. Was he being foolish? He'd called her and she hadn't called him back. Then again, maybe he hadn't yet said the correct words.

MAX CAUGHT UP with Terri in Kansas on Saturday afternoon. He was there in his new role as head of Rocksolid's NASCAR-related endeavors. He hadn't sought Terri out, but he found her in Bart's garage talking to her father. He happened to be in the vicinity—Billy Budd's garage wasn't too far away, as Billy was in the top twenty in points.

He took a moment to gaze at her without her noticing. She'd pulled her hair back into a ponytail and wore a PDQ ball cap on her head. She'd dressed in white tennis shoes, khaki pants and white polo shirt. She held a clipboard and was writing some information when he walked up.

"Hi," he said.

She turned, saw him and frowned. "What are you doing here?"

"Hoping we could talk," Max said.

"I'm helping my dad do some calculations."

"You can take a break," Philip said. He wiped his hands on a rag. "I have to go into the hauler and get a part, anyway."

Terri set the clipboard on a stack of tires. All around people bustled here and there. "I can spare you a few minutes."

"Thank you," Max replied.

He followed her out of the garage. She led him down to the snack bar. "This is as good as it gets," she said, gesturing to some tables.

She'd kept him somewhere public, but then, except for the Drivers' and Owners' lot, there were no real private spaces infield.

"I wanted to apologize. I overreacted," he said as they sat. "The only excuse I can give is that your actions injured my pride, and that I was a fool to have let them do so."

Terri nibbled on her bottom lip. "I'm sorry, too. I only wanted her out of our lives. After I left I realized something. You and I never set out to be serious. I mean, we were, but neither of us had any type of long-term goal in sight. You'd been burned by marriage and I'd broken off my engagement. But somewhere along the line, I fell in love with you and my priorities changed.

"I know you're not able to change. I know you'll never want marriage, and I discovered that I do. I don't want to be single for the rest of my days. I want what my parents have. Dating you was wonderful, but it's good we've split. That way I can move on. You've shown me I want more. I want everything. But I can't wait for something that's not going to happen."

"Oh." She'd floored him with her revelation. Max had thought they'd had things pretty good. How had they reached complacency so fast?

As he'd told Mandy at her party, marriage was complicated. Now Terri was telling him that because of words he'd uttered long ago, they had no future at all. It stung.

"Hey, Terri, you coming?" Bart Branch stood nearby with Anita.

"Yeah, hold on." She rose to her feet.

"Can we please keep talking about this?" Max asked. "What's your schedule? I can bend mine."

She shook her head. "Not necessary. I think we've said it all." With that she joined Bart and Anita and together the three moved toward Bart's hauler.

Max sat at the table longer, contemplating the mess he'd made of his life. Then he rose to his feet, checked his watch and headed for his next Rocksolid task.

"I THINK YOU'RE BEING stubborn," Bart told Terri later that night. They were sitting outside Bart's hauler, watching Will compete in his heat of racing battery-operated cars.

It was a little after eight, and the NASCAR Nationwide Series race had run earlier. The Kansas weather was mild, and the evening one of those where you just wanted to be outside, instead of cooped up indoors.

Terri sighed. She'd seen Max and walked away. He couldn't change, and she had.

"I told you what happened," Terri said, watching as Will's car edged past the front-runner. The guys were just as competitive on this miniature field as they'd be tomorrow.

"So?" Bart asked. "Terri, he's been self-sufficient all these years. You showed him there's something else he could have done. You made him feel rescued."

"That makes no sense," Terri said.

Bart's brow creased. "Yeah, it does. It's like me being in the car. You know, I think I'm a pro. But then you come along and say, 'If you'd only exercise more you could control your breathing,' and I'm thinking, what a crock. But you were right. Come on. We're guys. We don't like knowing we're not perfect, and hearing it from a woman just makes it worse."

"That sounds sexist."

"Maybe it is. Guys like Max are supposed to be the breadwinner and the protector."

Perhaps Bart was right. She and Max had both overreacted to the situation. Maybe they were still overreacting.

Perhaps she should talk to him some more, as he requested. Seeing him today had been devastating. As a man, Max was a gem. They'd loved each other. She'd wanted him heart and soul. She was a fool for walking away. Her mother's voice suddenly rang in Terri's ears. Love was more than being passionate. It was about being willing to work, especially when what you had was real.

Perhaps it was time for her to use the persistence she was known for and at least hash things out. She owed that to herself—and to her heart.

CHAPTER EIGHTEEN

ROCKSOLID HAD a suite for the race. Max had settled into his role and greeted his guests. The track was located just west of Kansas City, so the weekend's events were in honor of the year's top-grossing Midwest sales agents.

Billy Budd had stopped by the suite earlier and was now crossing the main stage in the infield for his driver introduction. Guests mingled, but Max didn't feel like socializing. However, he did his job. He took comfort from knowing he was good at what he did.

For the first time, though, uneasiness consumed him. He'd never been afraid of hard work or of being alone. But ever since Terri had walked into his life, she'd filled a chasm he'd been ignoring. She'd exposed the lies he'd been telling himself. He was lonely. Work didn't keep him warm or make him laugh. Work didn't love him. He could walk out of here and leave Barry, his second-in-command, in charge. Now that the race was about to start, no one would notice his absence.

Terri would be on the pit box today.

He gestured Barry over. "I need to take care of something. You got this?"

The younger man glanced around the room. He was also part of the Rising Stars Program. "I think so."

Max touched the credentials he wore around his neck. He had a "hot pass," allowing him access to the infield even once the race started. "It's easy. Make sure the food and drink don't run out and keep everyone happy. I'll be back before the race ends. I have something I must do."

TERRI MADE HER WAY to the pit box. The drivers were out on the track waving to the crowd. Once they finished everyone would line up for the national anthem and invocation. Then the drivers would climb into their cars and start their engines on the given command.

She saw him waiting for her. "Max!"

He stepped toward her. "I love you," he told her, not caring about the crew members who stood all around. "I'm not losing you."

"You're supposed to be in your suite. Your guests."

"They're fine. Don't you realize that you're more important than work? I love you. You make me complete. I don't want this to end."

"I…this isn't a good time." She didn't know what to say. Bart was walking toward them. She turned to her father, and he shook his head and stepped past her. She knew what that meant. The decision was hers to make.

"It's never going to be a good time," Max said. "Immediately after the race. Let's meet. Tonight. My house. The moment we both get back. No matter how late."

Terri glanced around. The track had been everything she loved—until Max. She smiled. "Okay."

He leaned forward and dropped a kiss on her cheek. "Thank you."

IT WAS MIDNIGHT before Terri reached Max's house. Justin Murphy had won the race and the mood on the PDQ plane had been subdued. Without a miracle, Bart was out of contention for the championship.

Max was waiting for her and he opened the door before her knock. "Hey," he said, letting her in. Now late September, the nights had gotten chilly. "Mandy's at my mom's. She has school tomorrow."

"She's not there on my account, is she?"

"No, mine. We had it scheduled before I left. I didn't want to wake her when I got back."

Terri took off her jacket and immediately stepped into Max's arms. He held her close and she inhaled his scent. "I don't ever want to go through this again. You're worth fighting for, Max."

"I don't want to fight," he said, drawing back so she could see the sincerity in his eyes.

"Me, neither, and that's not what I meant." They sat on the couch, and he drew her close. Strength and integrity emanated from him.

"We have to clear the air about Lola," Terri said. "I should have talked to you first, but right or wrong, my actions were rooted in love for you. I was not going to take any chance of losing you."

"I was an idiot," he said. "All you were doing was trying to help me out, so that we could have a future.

But I've been doing things for so long on my own that it's hard for me to rely on someone."

"We're a team," Terri said. "I'll try to be more patient in the future. I guess I expected you to be thrilled. I should monitor my own expectations."

"You should never expect less from me. I love you. And as for commitment, things change."

"They do. I'm not afraid. I love you. If you're the right man for me, and I know you are, I want a future with you. I don't want a promise of next weekend or next week. It has to be more than that."

"I agree. You know, Mandy wouldn't open the present from you until you came to see us. She wants you in our lives. So do I."

"So she's okay with all this?" Terri hoped so.

"She's been on me to marry you."

"You never planned on getting married again," Terri said. Her body tensed, but his tender smile was reassuring.

"I didn't, until I met you. I want you in my life forever, and I'm a traditional kind of guy."

"I'd hoped that," Terri said, about to burst with happiness as the final barrier to their being together crumbled. "So are you offering that?" Terri asked.

"Not yet," Max replied, drawing her closer still.

"You've lost me," she said haltingly.

Max kissed the end of her nose. "Yes, I want to marry you and I hope you want to marry me. I want to spend the rest of my life with you more than anything in the world. However, Mandy says I'm supposed to have flowers and a ring, and I don't have either. According to her, I'm also supposed to get down on one knee and be exceedingly romantic. And although she didn't come out and say it, she wants to be there."

Terri thought she was happy before, but now an all-encompassing joy settled over her. Max wanted to marry her. Mandy wanted her as a stepmother. "Mandy should probably be present if we're going to be a family."

Max kissed her lips once. "I want the proposal to be really special. Totally different from the last time. I hope you understand. You already know how I feel. I love you."

The fact that he wanted to make everything perfect created tears. She brushed them aside with the back of her hand. "I can wait until that special moment to give you my answer."

"As long as the answer is yes," Max said.

Terri's heart swelled and a few more tears fell before she could stop them. "What else would it be? Now kiss me again."

"Yes, ma'am." And Max lowered his mouth to hers.

EVEN THOUGH she was expecting a proposal, when Max surprised her by getting down on one knee in the Talladega infield, Terri's joy knew no bounds. She dropped to her knees and kissed him while Bart's entire team clapped, especially her dad. As Max slid a ring onto her finger, Mandy danced around like a kid with a new toy, her own happiness too much to contain.

"Guess you're going to get those grandchildren, after all," Bart teased Philip. "Just so long as you don't retire on me."

"Not a chance," Philip replied with a chuckle as he

watched his wife give Terri a hug. "I'll need somewhere to hide for at least a year as my wife plans Terri's wedding. She's been waiting a long time, so it'll be nuts at my house. I'll have to escape somewhere and tinker on cars. I might as well get paid for it."

"Thank goodness for that." Bart was in a good mood because, for the first time since the scandal broke, his mother had come to the track to watch him and Will race.

Terri caught Bart's gaze and winked at him, and then she lifted her lips to Max's for another kiss.

"And to think we met over a truck," Max teased as they rose to their feet and received the congratulations of those around them. "Still miss it?"

Terri glanced at the ring on her finger and hugged Mandy. She gazed at the man she loved. "Not one bit."

* * * * *

For more thrill-a-mile romances set against
the exciting backdrop of the NASCAR world,
don't miss:
HOT PURSUIT by Wendy Etherington
Available in September, 2008
For a sneak peek, just turn the page!

"I just don't get the PR rep thing. Grown men need somebody to follow them around everywhere they go, take care of them, handle all the details of their lives, direct them to every destination?" Sean said.

"Yes."

"Weird."

"The driver's job is to race. My job is to make their sponsor happy, so they will foot the bills for them to do their job. Which is to race. The caretaking is a side benefit." Kylie paused. "For them, not me."

"I don't think I'd like somebody following me around all day." He was the follower, not the followee. Grinning, Sean looked over at her. "Then again, if *you* were the one following me, I might not mind so much."

"That's a fairly inappropriate thing to say to the mother of one of your players."

Her lips were twitching, as if she might be holding back a laugh, but her eyes were narrowed—like her mother's had been earlier.

"If you'd go out with me, you wouldn't just be the mother of one of my players."

Her lips stopped twitching. She pressed them

together briefly. "I thought we settled this the other day."

"No, I temporarily set aside the topic to protect the boys."

"Protect the boys?"

"From seeing me beg to date you. I have a kick-butt reputation to maintain, you know."

She blinked slowly. "You're going to beg me to date you."

"If it's absolutely necessary."

"That won't be necessary."

"Really? I know weekends are out, but how about Tues—"

"That won't be necessary, because I'm not dating you."

"Why not?"

"You're my son's soccer coach."

"And dating you would violate my morality clause with the YMCA?"

"Don't be cute." She sighed. "Improbable, maybe even impossible for you, but try."

"I'll settle for irresistible."

She didn't return his smile. She crossed her arms over her chest. "I'm nearly a decade older than you."

"So?"

"Don't you want to date somebody your own age?"

"I want to date somebody I like. I like *you*."

"I like—" She stopped, biting her lip.

His heart rate sped up. "You like me, too."

"You're cute. Didn't I say you were cute? But I—" Grief settled over her face. She looked out the window. "I'm a widow. I'm not ready to date."

The age thing didn't worry him in the least. This obstacle, however, was much more dicey.

Though he'd resisted investigating Kylie, he'd done some digging into the life of her former husband, justifying his actions by saying the information was important in dealing with Ryan.

Matt Palmer had been an exceptional cop. Decorated and dedicated. Smart and tough when he needed to be. His death had been a blow not just to his family, but an entire squad and community.

"It's been four years," he said quietly. "You haven't dated at all?"

"A few times," she said to the window. "It hasn't gone well."

Sean pulled to a stop in the carpool line in front of Ryan's school. They barely knew each other. This conversation, touching on her sorrow and pain, was too personal, too much too soon.

His brother was right. Widows with kids weren't his style. Kylie was on a difficult emotional journey. Was he strong enough to help her down that road?

REQUEST YOUR FREE BOOKS!

2 FREE NOVELS PLUS 2 FREE GIFTS!

SPECIAL EDITION®

Life, Love and Family!

YES! Please send me 2 FREE Silhouette Special Edition® novels and my 2 FREE gifts (gifts are worth about $10). After receiving them, if I don't wish to receive any more books, I can return the shipping statement marked "cancel." If I don't cancel, I will receive 6 brand-new novels every month and be billed just $4.24 per book in the U.S. or $4.99 per book in Canada, plus 25¢ shipping and handling per book and applicable taxes, if any*. That's a savings of at least 15% off the cover price! I understand that accepting the 2 free books and gifts places me under no obligation to buy anything. I can always return a shipment and cancel at any time. Even if I never buy another book from Silhouette, the two free books and gifts are mine to keep forever.

235 SDN EEYU 335 SDN EEY6

Name _____ (PLEASE PRINT)

Address _____ Apt. #

City _____ State/Prov. _____ Zip/Postal Code

Signature (if under 18, a parent or guardian must sign)

Mail to the **Silhouette Reader Service:**
IN U.S.A.: P.O. Box 1867, Buffalo, NY 14240-1867
IN CANADA: P.O. Box 609, Fort Erie, Ontario L2A 5X3

Not valid to current subscribers of Silhouette Special Edition books.

Want to try two free books from another line?
Call 1-800-873-8635 or visit www.morefreebooks.com.

* Terms and prices subject to change without notice. N.Y. residents add applicable sales tax. Canadian residents will be charged applicable provincial taxes and GST. Offer not valid in Quebec. This offer is limited to one order per household. All orders subject to approval. Credit or debit balances in a customer's account(s) may be offset by any other outstanding balance owed by or to the customer. Please allow 4 to 6 weeks for delivery. Offer available while quantities last.

Your Privacy: Silhouette is committed to protecting your privacy. Our Privacy Policy is available online at www.eHarlequin.com or upon request from the Reader Service. From time to time we make our lists of customers available to reputable third parties who may have a product or service of interest to you. If you would prefer we not share your name and address, please check here. ☐

SSE08R